Taking What's His

a Shillings Agency novel

Diane Alberts

Entangled Publishing, LLC
2614 South Timberline Road
Suite 109
Fort Collins, CO 80525
Visit our website at www.entangledpublishing.com.

Brazen is an imprint of Entangled Publishing, LLC. For more information on our titles, visit www.brazenbooks.com.

Edited by Heather Howland
Cover design by Heather Howland
Cover art by Shutterstock

Manufactured in the United States of America

First Edition April 2015

This one goes to all the Whovians out there. And if you're not one yet…what are you waiting for? Join the dark side. We have cookies, bowties, and fezzes.

Chapter One

Holt Cunningham sat at the crowded bar, staring into his empty glass, and couldn't help but wonder how the hell he'd gotten there, and if he'd ever feel normal again. A year ago, he'd been in combat, kicking ass and taking names. There hadn't been anything to worry about except avoiding bullets. He'd been invincible. Undefeatable.

And then…he'd been defeated.

All it had taken was one well placed IED and *bam*. His whole life had changed in an instant. He wasn't a Marine anymore, everyone from his platoon was dead, and now he was a fucking IT guy at Shillings Agency.

He had no idea what to do with the rest of his fucking life. He couldn't sleep more than an hour without waking up in a fucking cold sweat. Barely ate. The only things that filled the empty void inside of him that screamed out in agony were meaningless one-night stands and booze, but even those had stopped working recently.

That wouldn't stop him from trying again, though.

He was a stubborn ass like that.

The door opened, and the cold winter's night air hit him. He huddled closer to the bar. "Welcome to fucking Maine," he muttered.

The bartender came up. "Hey. Where'd your friend go?"

His friend and co-worker at the agency, Gordon Waybrook, had tossed back a drink and then left. He'd been down in the dumps over some princess chick that wouldn't marry him. Why any man would want to get married was beyond Holt, but to each his own.

"He had to go." Holt pushed his glass across the bar. "I'll have another."

The bartender, Mike, tightened his lips. "You don't look so good, man. Maybe you should call it quits and go home."

"If I wanted an evaluation, I'd go to a...to a...shrink." He gripped the edge of the bar tightly, angry that the word had eluded him. "I didn't. I came to a bar. Now get me my drink."

Mike jerked the glass away. "We might be friends, but that doesn't give you an excuse to be a dick. One more, and then I'm cutting you off."

Holt watched him go, already regretting his words. "I'm sorry," he whispered to no one, since Mike had already left. That was something that was messed up in his head, too. He didn't think things through before speaking. What was the point, when nine times out of ten his words still came out all messed up?

Someone sat beside him, and he glanced over. It was a woman with strawberry blonde hair. She was slim and short, and she smelled like flowers. He couldn't make out her face, but her profile looked gorgeous. She had a small, pert nose and high cheekbones. Her lashes were long and thick. Everything about her drew his gaze, and he couldn't look away.

As soon as she settled, she turned and smiled at him. He froze, all intelligent words leaving his brain as well as his mouth. She was…she was…

Beautiful. She was utterly *beautiful*.

And totally not for him. He'd ruin a sweet thing like her in seconds.

Her bright hazel eyes met his without hesitance, and when she smiled, two dimples popped out. Her whole face lit up, too. She looked young, but not too young to be in a bar. "Hey," she said.

He blinked at her. Her voice was magically soft, as if she was singing instead of talking, and he couldn't think of a single word to say back. So he just stared at her.

Mike came over, saving Holt from replying. As soon as he set down the drink, the bartender turned to the beauty next to him. "What'll you have?"

"An appletini, please," she said.

Holt grabbed his drink and stared at it, his heart thumping in his chest, as Mike carded her. He went off to get her order, so she must have been of age, but she couldn't be much older than twenty-one. She was too fresh faced. Too pure.

A piercing pain hit him, and he winced.

"Hey. Are you okay?" she asked, her voice soft with concern. "Did you have one too many, maybe?"

He wished that were his fucking problem. Turning to her, he tightened his grip on his glass. He was determined not to let his vocabulary slip, and to send her running as quickly as possible. A girl like her shouldn't be around a guy like him. He was no good. "Yes. I'm fine."

"Okay." She smiled. "How are you tonight?"

Feeling like a bastard. "I'm…fine. You?"

"Awful." She dropped the side of her head on her hand, facing him, and smiled. Jesus, she was too gorgeous to be talking to someone like him. "I've had a really bad couple of days, to be honest."

That seemed to be going around. Instead of snarling back at her to scare her away, like he should have, he wanted to…help her. Make her feel better. "What happened?"

"Well…" She stared down at the bar. "My boyfriend of two months slept with my old college roommate the other day, for starters."

Fucking prick. Anyone who would do that to someone as sweet-faced as her deserved a punch to the nuts. So she was single, then. But she still had a roommate. That screamed of college or some shit like that. How old *was* she? "Then he's an asshole."

"Why do you say that?" she asked, blinking at him.

"You're stunning. That means he must be a fool — and an asshole." He shrugged. "Obviously."

"Aw." Her smile lit up her face again. "You're sweet."

Sweet. That was the last thing he was. He was a fucking hot mess, and he should really let her know that before she got the wrong idea. "No. I'm not. You—"

"If you say so." She waved a hand as if swatting away a fly. It was adorable. "But, anyway, he was probably upset because I wouldn't put out."

That was a hell of a lot of information to give a stranger, but she seemed the open type. And it only made him like her more, which had him saying: "Then he's a prick, as well as a fool. Are you upset?"

"No, more angry than anything." She glanced over her shoulder, licked her lips, and turned back to him. "You seem like a really nice guy. So, uh, can I ask you a huge favor that's highly inappropriate?"

Seeing as he'd barely said two words to her, he had no idea how she'd decided he was a *nice guy*. If she knew who he was, and what he'd done, she would never have fucking called him that. Or sweet. "Uh…"

"Okay, this is going to sound crazy, but I'm going to go for it." She leaned in and rested her hand directly next to his. Her cheeks flushed bright red. "Can you kiss me?"

He gripped his drink tighter, because, man, he wanted to. He shouldn't want to, but damn it, he *did*. "Jesus. Do you come on to all the men in…in…bars like this?"

"No, but you see, he's here. My ex. And he's watching me. Well, us, technically." She watched him through her long red lashes. "And he looks jealous because I'm with you, which makes me happy."

He glanced over his shoulder. Sure enough, some blond haired dude stood in the corner, watching them. He looked pissed as hell. He couldn't be more than twenty-three. Maybe. "That's him?"

"Yeah."

The boy in question looked like one of those football quarterbacks who'd owned the high school hallways and everyone in them. A total douche who wouldn't know where a woman's G-spot was if you gave him a fucking compass and a map. "You could do better."

She flushed and bit down on her lower lip. "Thanks. I'm

trying right now."

He wasn't better, and she was crazy if she thought he was. Crazier than he was. But even so, he wanted to be that guy for her, wanted to be *nice*. But kissing her wasn't really what a nice guy would do, was it?

Not when he was as fucked up in the head as Holt was.

He gripped his glass tighter. "You could do better than me, too. Trust me."

"I disagree." She eyed him, nibbling on her lower lip. "Please?"

Fuuuck, she had the damsel in distress thing down pat. And she might not know it, but he'd never been good at ignoring a woman in need. All it took was a well placed *please* and a flutter of the lashes and he crumbled. That, at least, hadn't changed in the war. And while he might not be good at all the things he used to be good at, there was one thing he still excelled at.

Seducing a woman.

And she'd damn well *asked* for it. But before he found out if her lips tasted as sweet as they looked, he had a few questions. "How old are you?"

Her cheeks pinked. "Twenty-three. I just finished grad school." She licked her lips. "You?"

Of-fucking-course. She was practically a baby, damn it. He shouldn't kiss her. Couldn't. He needed to send her running for the hills. "Twenty-seven. Too old for a sweet little girl like you. You need to—"

She rolled her eyes. "Hardly. He's coming. *Please*."

Damn it, she'd done it again. He shifted in his seat, watching her asshole ex. He started heading their way, frowning. All the reasons he had for not kissing her—her age, his impending migraine, the adorable innocence that made him want to protect her—faded away. The jerk needed to see that she was no longer his. "Do you want me to kiss you so you can get him back, or to show you've moved on?"

"Move on, for sure. There's no way I'll go back to—"

Curling his hand behind her neck, he hauled her close and melded his mouth to hers, cutting her off. As soon as their lips touched, everything seemed to fall into place. It was as if she was a pill he'd taken, and she'd cured him.

The anger, the confusion, the pain, the fear.

It all quieted inside his head, to be replaced by the way she felt against him.

He knew without a doubt, the instant his mouth touched hers, she was different from all the other women he'd kissed. She could make him different, too. That didn't make any sense…and yet it did. It really fucking did.

Damned if she didn't kiss like a woman who didn't have much experience with this type of thing, and it was refreshingly sweet. She gasped into his mouth, her hands resting on his chest, and he took advantage of the opening she'd given him. Slipping his tongue between her lips, he found hers and swept across it.

Her fingers fisted his shirt, and she moaned.

It was the sexiest moan he'd ever motherfucking heard.

Deepening the kiss, he slid his hand down to the small of her back and drew her closer to him. His whole hand splayed across her from end to end, she was that damn tiny. Almost hesitantly, her hands moved up, curling over his shoulders to latch on to him for dear life. She tasted heavenly, as if she was made just for him.

And she felt like it, too.

He'd kissed a lot of women, but he'd never kissed like *this*. And a kiss had never made him feel so damn unsettled before. It was as if some invisible force was pushing them together, and nothing he did or said would change the fact that by the end of the night...she'd be naked in his bed. The bizarre desire to pick her up, throw her over his shoulder, and carry her out of the bar, ass up in the air, hit him like a fist to the gut.

He ended the kiss, because even though he might not know her, he knew one thing for sure. She was the type of woman who deserved more than a one-night stand, and he couldn't give it to her. So it was time to send her running away...for real this time.

She moaned in protest and strained to get closer. "More," she whispered.

"Uh uh." He pressed a finger to her lips, grinning at her cockily, as if she hadn't just fucked with his head with an innocent kiss. "You want any more, you need to walk out that door with me right now. Come home with me. I swear I can give you a hell of a lot more than a chaste kiss in a bar. And it'll make him hurt even more, too."

He'd bet his life that she wasn't the type to leave a bar with a strange man, so if that didn't make her babble a few quickly strewn together reasons she had to go back to her friends, then he'd wear a pink dress to work tomorrow.

She blinked at him, her plump pink lips wet and swollen. "That was *chaste*? Are you kidding me?"

"Yep. You have no idea what I'm capable of." He trailed his hand down her thigh, something he'd never usually do without a clear invitation. But he wanted to save her from himself, before it was too late, and if she didn't reject him...

he wouldn't be able to walk away. He wanted her. "Come home with me, though, and I'll show you, baby."

He threw that last part in for good measure.

No woman liked being called *baby*.

"Uh…" Glancing over her shoulder at her ex, she pressed her lips together. This was when she would, and should, tell him to kiss her ass, then spin off of the stool and run back to her safe little friends in the corner, who he could see watching them with open mouths. "You know what? Sure. Let's go."

He forced a smirk. "That's what I—" He cut himself off, her words finally registering. "Wait. What?"

She stood and held out her hand. "I said, *yes*."

Well, shit. Now what the fuck was he supposed to do?

He didn't own any pink dresses.

Chapter Two

Lydia Thomas took a deep breath and smiled at the guy who'd invited her back to his place, ignoring the voices in her head shouting at her to change her mind about this whole thing. To play it safe. Life was full of choices, and she'd always taken the straight road, instead of the one less travelled. Always made the "right" choice. But not tonight. Not here. His dark hair and scruffy face screamed of danger and passion, two things she'd never had much of in her life. But the glasses he wore…ah, they were nerdy.

And not dorky nerdy, but *hot* nerdy.

She normally wasn't the type to take chances, let alone go home with strange men, but she'd never met a man who was a contradiction at its finest, who made her *want* to go home with him on the first night. She'd spent her whole life waiting for the perfect guy, the one who would cherish her and love her forever, and who would make her feel as if she'd die if he didn't take her. One who would sweep her off her feet and make her feel like a princess.

After countless failed attempts at finding her Prince Charming among the Horny Harrys…it was time to stop. Just stop. She'd always been the type to fall too fast, too easily, but she'd managed to kill that habit over the last year by taking things slow. Too slow, according to her jerk of an ex. So, yeah, maybe she was taking a step backwards by going home with this guy within minutes of meeting him.

But she didn't intend to fall in love with him…

I just want to fall into his bed.

If she'd learned anything in her quest for love, and her past penchant for falling too easily, she'd learned one thing: The perfect guy didn't exist. Men nowadays were raw, real, and mostly greedy. It was time she tried lowering her expectations for a short moment. It was time to stop hunting for a prince. To stop waiting for the guy who would sweep her off her feet with his words and his touch…and go home with the guy who made her *want*.

And she'd finally found that guy.

Being good was boring. It was time to have a little fun.

"Excuse me?" the guy said. He looked vaguely familiar, but she couldn't put her finger on why, or how. And she didn't *care* why, either. "I don't think I heard you correctly."

She fought back a smile. The dude seemed shocked she'd said yes, but hey, to be fair, so was she. "Oh, you heard me well enough," she said, losing herself in his dark blue eyes. It took all her concentration to carry on a conversation with him, when all she could think about was kissing him again. "I said, let's go."

He stared at her with an amusing mixture of surprise and desire. It was even more perfectly clear that when he'd made that invitation, he hadn't expected her to accept. But there was something about this guy that demanded submission. That demanded she go home with him, have the time of her life, and leave with a limp and a smile on her face in the morning. This guy could give her both those things.

On the surface, he looked like a nerdy, hot dude in glasses and a checkered shirt. Like he was more at home sitting on his couch playing his Xbox One, than sitting in a bar. She'd bet too many women wrote him off that way, too. But she'd been surrounded by two geek brothers and all their friends her whole life. And one thing she learned by eavesdropping—as younger sisters do—outside their doors? Geeks were the dirtiest, freakiest, *sexiest* men of them all. Hands down. And this guy might be the king of them all.

He stood up, towering over her, and dragged a hand through his hair. It spiked naturally as an aftereffect. "My ride's out front."

As he rummaged in his wallet, she studied him from underneath her lashes. He was six-foot-three, easily, and he had dark auburn hair and even darker blue eyes. He seemed to be the type of guy that was persistently just a little bit scruffy, and it suited him. Just like those khakis that hugged his butt.

He reeked of dark, stormy, addictive sex, and she was ready to collect.

Tossing a twenty on the bar, he turned back to her with a penetrating stare—as if he saw why she was going home with him, and understood better than she herself did. Which, of course, made no sense at all. His long, lean body wasn't overly muscular, but she could tell that he was stronger than he appeared. She could see it in the hardness of his arms, and the way he carried himself. He was a man accustomed to physical activity.

"Ready?" he asked.

Nope. "Oh yeah." She started for the door, but he rushed past her and opened it before she could do it for herself. So. He was a gentleman, too. This guy was an enigma she longed to unwrap...one article of clothing at a time. "Thank you, Mister...?"

He cocked a brow at her. "If you're going home with me, I think you can use my first name."

"Fine. I'm Lydia."

"I'm Holt."

And just like that, she knew why she recognized him. He was her older brother Steven's friend. They worked at the same private security agency, and Steven had posted a few pictures of them together on Facebook. Every time she'd seen him, she'd been unable to glance away. There was just something that had caught her attention on the screen, so it was no wonder he'd caught her attention in real life, too.

"Oh my God. I know—" She cut herself off in the nick of time.

If she told him who she was, would he end their night together right here in the parking lot? She had no idea how close her brother and Holt were, but she had a feeling their bro code would make him leave the bar alone, and she didn't want him to back off. She wanted him to get *on*.

He ran his finger over her jawline. "What do you know?"

"Uh...nothing. Nothing at all."

Watching her closely, he let out a soft laugh. "You know nothing at all? I find that hard to believe."

"Do you go to that bar often?"

He shook his head, still smiling. "That's the worst pickup

line ever, and you're a horrible subject changer."

"That's not entirely accurate. I already picked you up," she pointed out, her heart racing. "So I must be doing something right."

"Some might argue that I'm the one who picked you up."

"No way. I asked you to kiss me," she said quickly, glancing up at him. In the moonlight, he looked even darker. Even sexier, too. "So I made the first move."

"I disagree. I always make the first move, and this was no fucking exception. I agreed to kiss you, so that was my first move." He walked her around the side of the building and spun her so her back rested against it, capturing her hands by her head. For a second, fear hit her hard in the gut. But then he pressed his body against hers, and fear became desire. So. Much. Desire. "And this is the second."

Her breath whooshed out of her lungs. "Oh?"

"Tell me what you're doing out here, alone, with me." He trailed his hand down her jawline, his touch as soft as a misty rain on a spring day, and yet as sharp as a razor's edge, too. "You can't possibly think going home with me is better than going home alone, just because some prick broke your heart. I'm trying to be a good guy here…"

"I want to go home with you," she said, laughing. "Why is that so hard to believe?"

His jaw tightened. "You have no idea how dangerous a guy like me can be."

Her heart picked up speed, but she wasn't sure what from—the desire his dominant words brought out in her, or the intimidation that he'd managed to hold over her head. He was *good*. "Why are you dangerous?"

"Why would you think I wasn't?" His fingers skimmed over her cleavage. Her neckline was chaste and high, so he had to dip his fingers under her shirt to do so. "I went to that bar, looking for a good fuck, like always, and you sat next to me. That makes me opportunistic, but it doesn't make me a good guy."

She lifted her chin. "I came looking for the same thing. I sat next to you for a reason." *Liar, liar, pants on fire.* She hadn't, but then she'd seen him. She couldn't think of a better guy to spend the night with than Holt. "So…there."

"I don't believe you. You said your boyfriend of two months broke up with you because you didn't put out." He gripped the tip of her chin, latching onto her gaze. "That tells me you don't jump into bed with just any guy. You don't even know me. And yet, here we are, and you're ready to fuck me without a second thought. I'm not usually one to question such things, but with you…I am. I want to know you're certain."

"I didn't sleep with him, no." Her cheeks heated, and she pressed her thighs together. It was on the tip of her tongue to admit who she was to him, and why that made her more comfortable to take a chance on him, but she didn't want to risk it. "That doesn't mean I don't want to do it with you, though."

"Why?"

"You make me want to. Okay?" She blew out a frustrated breath. "You make me want you, so I'm going to take you. Is that such a horrible thing? Does there *need* to be more?"

His grip on her hands flexed, and he slipped his thigh in between hers. His mouth pressed against her pulse, sending her BPM through the roof. "Nope. But, squeezing your hot little legs together won't make your pussy feel better. You need me for that."

Her stomach clenched tight. He'd said…he…oh my God, that was hot. She'd known that underneath those glasses was a bad boy who knew exactly what to do with a good girl like her. "*Holt.*"

"Yeah?" he asked, nibbling on her lower neck.

"Take me home with you."

"Abso-fucking-lutely." He pushed off the wall, and she immediately missed his touch. It was electrifying. "Come with me."

He placed a hand on her lower back and steered her toward the last row of cars. In the middle was a dark grey Toyota Prius. It had *Doctor Who* stickers all over it, and a TARDIS on the side, too. It was totally the type of car she could picture a guy like Holt driving. She stopped beside it.

Stumbling a bit, he stopped and blinked at her.

After a moment, he opened his mouth, and closed it. As if he was trying to gather his thoughts. "Did you want to drive to my place separately or something?"

"Um…" What a weird question. Why would she want to drive his car? "No. I didn't drive here, so I don't have a car with me."

"Okay." He blinked at her again. "Then why are we standing here?"

"Because it's your car?"

His eyes narrowed. "No, it's not. Mine's the red truck at the end."

"But…oh." Her cheeks heated. "I'm sorry. I just, uh—"

He pointed at it. "You assumed I drove an environment friendly roller skate with *Doctor Who* stickers plastered all over it?"

"Y-Yes?"

He snorted. "Not fucking likely. I don't put stickers on my truck, not even for the Doctor. It damages the paint."

She latched onto that last part. "But you *do* like *Doctor Who*?"

"Of course." He led her toward the truck at the end. "Do you?"

"Uh, yeah. What's not to like?"

He stopped walking. "Seriously?"

"Yeah. Ten is my favorite, but eleven is a close sec—"

Growling, he threw her up against his truck, his mouth closing over hers hungrily. She gasped and parted her lips, which he took full advantage of. His tongue brushed up against hers, and he made the sexiest sound she'd ever heard in her life. She fisted her hands on his shirt, tugging him closer, and he gave her what she wanted.

And then he gave her even more.

His hand slipped between her legs, brushing against her core exactly where she needed him most, and even through her jeans the result was electrifying. How had he *known*? His mouth moved over hers at the same time as his fingers did, hard and fast. She'd kissed plenty of guys here and there—okay, fine. Five. But still—she'd been kissed before, and she'd even had sex.

But she'd never felt like *this*.

There was no stopping the immense pleasure he brought to life with his touch. It crashed through her, intense and fast. He muffled her moans with his mouth, his fingers circling and swirling and—*oh my God*. Her nails dug into her palms, even through his shirt, and she stiffened. Stars erupted in front of her eyes, and an inescapable pleasure surged over her whole body. So...*that* was an orgasm. "Holt, oh my God."

"I'm here." He chuckled and broke off the kiss, his lips a breath from hers. "That was so fucking cute."

Shoot. Me. Now. "*Cute*? Did you seriously call my orgasm *cute*?"

Oh, God. He laughed even harder. "I get it. I know why you're coming home with me now. You're horny as fuck, and so am I. So let's go."

He latched hands with her and led her around to the passenger side of his truck. After he opened the door for her, he lifted her up and set her in the seat as if she didn't weigh anything at all. He closed the door behind her with a wink, and strode around the back of the truck whistling. He'd just given her her first orgasm *ever*, had no clue who she was, and was whistling as if he didn't have a care in the world. She was ready to pounce on him and demand he give her more. Lots more.

He opened the door and climbed into his truck, starting it with a twist of his wrist. "Buckle up."

She blinked at him. "What?"

"Buckle." He clicked his seatbelt. "Up. *Now*."

"Oh. Right." Blinking, she shook her head and did as told. As soon as it clicked, he threw his arm over her seat and backed up. He looked as cool as a cucumber, without a single tremor to be seen, and she was a quivering mess. "Why did you...do that?"

"Make you come?" he asked, his lips quirked into a small smile. "Isn't that kind of why we're going to my place?"

Her cheeks heated. "Well, yeah. But why here?"

"You started talking nerdy to me." He shrugged. "I liked

it, so I rewarded you."

Rewarded her? "Oh, I've got plenty more where that came from." She grinned. "My favorite moment with Ten and Rose is when—"

His fingers flexed on the wheel, and his jaw tensed. Gone was the teasing smile he'd worn moments before. He shot her a commanding look, his jaw line hard and unyielding. "Save it for my place."

Part of her wanted to keep going. Tease him some more. But the other part of her instinctually sensed the power leashed underneath the words. And that part of her obeyed without question. "Yes, sir."

"Yeah." His fingers flexed even more. "You'll be calling that out later, too."

Her stomach tightened, and she clenched her fists in her lap. "Holt."

"Lydia."

The way he said her name… "I'm not going to call you *sir*."

Smirking, he adjusted his grip on the wheel. "Yeah. You will."

Instead of answering, she swallowed hard and kept silent. The way he said it…yeah, it made her think he was right. And that was equal parts thrilling and scary. His dark auburn hair reflected the streetlights, and so did his dark blue eyes. And when he smiled, she could see dimples underneath his sexy scruff. Not that he was smiling now. Instead, he looked determined.

Beneath it all, his gaze held a sadness to them she'd never seen before. What had put that shadow in his eyes? Where had he been? What had he seen? She was dying to know.

Almost as much as she was dying to kiss him again.

He stopped in front of a house. It was two-story brick colonial, fairly large, and it looked like the type of place a guy in his twenties wouldn't step foot in.

She stared at it. "Is this your house?"

"Yeah." He shut off the truck and jumped out of it. She opened her door and hopped down, landing on both feet. He was there waiting for her. How had he moved so fast? "But we have to be quiet. My mom's sleeping upstairs. I live in the basement."

She froze. "Oh my—"

"I'm kidding." He burst into laughter, holding his stomach. "You're so fucking gullible. It's adorable."

Her cheeks went hot. "I am not."

"Yeah, you are." He grabbed her hand and pulled her toward the door. "But only about this, because you seem to think I'm a gamer geek who never grew up or moved out of his parent's house."

Okay. He was right. She totally had pre-conceived opinions about him, but she also knew that under that facade, he was more. "I'm sorry."

He lifted a shoulder. "Nothing to be sorry for. I don't give a fuck."

"So…about that gullibility thing. You were kidding about the whole 'sir' thing, too, then, weren't you?"

He shook his head. "Hell no."

"But I—" *Don't know how I feel about that yet*. She cut herself off when he opened the door and motioned her inside.

As she walked into the living room, hugging herself, she glanced around. The house was pleasantly furnished.

Modern, with a hint of elegance. Not a single Darth Vader suit to be found. Not even a single cosplay outfit. It looked nothing like she'd expected. *You're outta your league, here, Lydia.*

"Want a drink?" he asked, hanging his keys on the hook by the door. There were four hooks, but only one set of keys. "I have pretty much anything you'd want."

She set her purse down in the foyer. "Do you have white wine?"

"Moscato okay?"

"Yeah. That's great." She followed him into the kitchen, greedily eating up every single detail of his home. "You have a nice place."

"Thanks." He pulled out two wine glasses, falling silent. She got the impression, again, that he was thinking over his next words. He seemed to do that a lot. "I bought it sight unseen when I moved here for my job."

"What do you do?"

He poured the wine with a less than steady hand. "I'm an IT guy. Go ahead. Laugh. Stereotypes and all that shit."

"I'm not going to laugh," she said softly, taking the full glass he handed her. "Heck, I don't even have a job yet, so I'm certainly not going to laugh at someone who does."

He filled his own glass, and raised it in a toast. They both drank. "What did you go to college for?"

She wasn't sure how much Steven had talked about her, but she answered honestly anyway. She might not want to tell him who she was, but she wasn't about to *lie* to him. She wasn't a liar. There just wasn't a reason to complicate things between them. She'd been waiting for a guy like him to come along and awaken her urges, so to speak.

And now he was here.

They'd have their fun, and then they'd never see each other again. He was work-buddies with her brother. It wasn't as if there would be awkward family dinners afterward or anything. He'd never even have to know he'd slept with his friend's little sister. The bro code would remain intact.

"I got my nursing degree." She sipped her wine. "I just graduated from St. Joseph's, and I'm currently trying to find a good OR nurse position…and failing."

"Ah." He stepped closer, towering over her. He smelled so good. She didn't know what type of cologne he wore, but she'd never smelled it before. "I'll let you know if I hear of any openings."

She took another big gulp of wine. He wouldn't be around in her life long enough for that, so it was an empty promise and they both knew it. "Thanks."

"But for now," he paused and rubbed his jaw. "Let's talk expectations for tonight."

"Okay…"

"One night. That's all I ever offer anyone." He tugged on her hair. It sent tingles shooting through her veins, and she got lost in his dark blue eyes. His glasses framed them perfectly. "One wild, crazy night, and then we both move on. No broken hearts. No painful goodbyes."

She laughed uneasily. "I don't need you to define the perimeters of a one-night stand. It's not exactly rocket science."

"Fair enough." His lips twitched. "Just making sure we're on the same page, is all. I can't afford to have someone get hurt because they mistook something I said in that bed—and trust me, I'll say a lot—as some kind of promise or shit like that."

"Oh, we are." She downed the rest of her wine and set it down, then took a step toward him. Gently, she undid the top button of his dark shirt. "I'll leave here and never bother you again, *sir*. I promise."

"That's another thing," he said, cupping her jaw. His touch was light, but it stopped her in her tracks. It was… possessive. Domineering, too. "You say it in a joking manner, but I'm dead fucking serious about this. I like it when you call me sir. I like to play rough in bed. Do you?"

She had no idea, but if it was what he liked, then she'd roll with it until she didn't like it anymore. She'd tried the *sir* on for size earlier, and it had felt good, so why not? "Yeah. Of course I do."

"You're just full of surprises, aren't you, Lydia?" He tugged her hair harder, not stopping until they were chest to chest. He skimmed his hand down her arm, and she shivered. "One last question."

Her stomach clenched tight. "Yeah?"

"I need to know…" His hand slipped between her legs, and he urged them apart. She did what he wanted, her breath catching in her throat when he stepped between them. He rolled his hips up, rubbing his huge erection against her core. "Just how rough do you like it?"

She tipped her chin up and did her best to look sure of herself, when she wasn't sure of anything anymore. "I-I'm very open. Do what you normally do, and I'll let you know if you go too far."

"Well then…" He tightened his grip on her. "Hands on the wall. *Now*."

Chapter Three

Holt watched her closely. If she showed any sign of nerves, or doubt, he'd back off. Have a normal night of sex with a normal girl, and then say goodbye come morning. He'd done it plenty of times. It wasn't as if he needed to be in control in the bedroom or anything. He just did it for fun, when the right girl came along.

Something told him she was the right kind of girl.

Without a word, she spun around, looked over her shoulder at him, and placed her hands on the wall. Her lids drifted shut, and she bit her bottom lip. "Holt."

Fuck, he loved the way she said his name. All hot, sexy, and needy. He stepped up behind her, gripping her hips. She fit his hand perfectly. "Yeah?"

He'd quit calling her baby after he'd quit trying to make her see she shouldn't go home with a guy like him. He might know she was making a mistake, but she seemed determined to make it. And if she was going to go home with someone, it might as well be him. At least he could get her off, unlike her loser ex.

"Wh-What would you like me to do now, sir?"

His breath escaped in a long groan, and he slid his hands over her curves, exploring each and every one. As his hands moved up over her sides, she held her breath. The second he closed his palms over her breasts, she exhaled and let out a soft moan.

Damn, she was so fucking hot. So ready.

"Now, you stand there and do everything I say, without question." He rolled his thumbs over her hard nipples, forming his next words carefully. "And maybe…maybe I'll reward you for being a good girl."

She dropped her head back on his shoulder, a tiny sigh escaping her. He stared down at her face, memorizing every soft detail. The way her lashes curved over her cheekbones. Her plump, red lips. The strawberry blonde eyebrows that contrasted with her smooth, porcelain skin. She reminded him of…

Shit, he couldn't quite place it.

Shaking his head, he forced his thoughts out of his mind, and focused on the present. The very real, beautiful, *hot* present that currently moaned in his arms. He trailed his fingers up her arms, trapping her palms between his and the wall when she tried to move them. While holding her in place, he nibbled on her throat, biting down with enough pressure to sting a little bit.

Damn if she didn't taste like fucking heaven, too.

"Don't move until I say you can," he growled, letting go of her. "Understood?"

She didn't move. "Yes, sir."

He ran his hands over her soft skin, tensing when she let out a sexy as fuck moan. He traced her curves, letting his fingers memorize her body, and then when he reached the hem of her shirt, he balled it in his fist. "This needs to go. *Now*."

She nodded frantically. "Do it. Take it off."

*Tsk*ing, he shook his head. "You're not the one giving out the orders." Inch by slow inch, he pulled her shirt up until it snagged on her arms. "You may lift your arms for me."

Her arms raised above her head, and she shot him a teasing look. "Like this?"

"Fucking perfect." He yanked her shirt over her head and tossed it. Without wasting a second, he undid the clasp of her bra. Skimming his fingertips over her bare skin, he lowered her arms down to her sides, threading his fingers with hers. She seemed pretty damn steady, but he had to ask. "You're certain?"

She bit down on her lip and nodded once. "Y-Yes."

"Then you're mine for the rest of the night." His grip on her flexed, and he nibbled on the bare skin at the base of her neck. Her bra hung off her shoulders, but he didn't remove it yet. He liked to unwrap his presents slowly. "All. Fucking. Mine."

A small, fragile sounding moan escaped her. It made him want to cradle her close and protect her from everything and everyone. Even him.

Hell, *especially* him.

He slid his hands up, touching every inch of smooth skin as he went along, and slipped his fingers under the straps of her bra. The tips of her dusky nipples were visible over the top, and he couldn't look away. Delicious.

There was no other way to describe her.

He flicked his fingers and the bra fell to the floor, landing at her feet. She shuddered and raised her arms, as if to cover herself, and he growled. "*Don't.*"

She shivered, freezing instantly. "Whatever you say, sir."

It was obvious that she got off on him being bossy while seducing her. So he roughened his voice even more and said, "I didn't tell you to move. Hands on the fucking wall, *now*."

"S-Sorry." She slammed them in place, her shoulders rising and falling with each ragged breath. "You're killing me."

"I haven't even started yet." A small laugh escaped him, and he gripped the waist of her jeans. "Not even close."

"Oh my God," she moaned, dropping her forehead on the wall.

He hadn't given her permission to do that, but he let it slide. She'd said she liked to play rough, but something told him she didn't have much experience actually *doing* it. Maybe she'd fantasized, or read that *Fifty Shades of Whatever* book that all women fawned over, but she didn't seem to actually know what she was getting herself into. That was fine. He'd just have to take it slow with her.

They had all night. And he'd never wanted to take his time exploring a woman's body more than he did hers. He'd relish in every inch of skin he uncovered. Every sigh, moan, and cry. By the time he was finished with her, she'd never be the same again.

But for the first time, he worried *he* might not be, either.

Ignoring the warning voices whispering in his head that said this woman was different, he gently undid the button of her jeans and slid his fingers inside her pants. She wore a tiny scrap of satin underneath those jeans, and she was soft and shaved. Cupping her from behind, he rubbed his palm against her clit.

She moaned and curled her hands into fists. "*Holt.*"

"Yeah?" he breathed into her ear, pressing his lips to the soft shell. "You need more?"

"Yes. More." She bit down on her lip. "So much more."

Yeah. Me too. "Hmm." He sank to his knees and removed his hand. "Not yet."

A frustrated sound escaped her. "Oh my freaking God. I'm going to kill—"

"I suggest you stop that threat right there."

She slammed her mouth shut. "*Fine.*"

"What's that? I didn't hear you. I believe the proper response is, 'yes, sir.'"

Mutinously, she glared down at him.

He palmed her ass, squeezing her through her jeans. Experimentally, he slapped her. She jumped, her cheeks flushing with color. "Say it."

She licked her lips. "Or what?"

"I'll spank your ass until you can't sit down without thinking about me, and what I did to this hot little body of yours tonight."

Staring down at him, she said nothing.

With one quick jerk, he pulled her pants down and closed his palm over her. Damn if she didn't fit perfectly in his hands, too. If he were the sentimental type, he'd say she'd been made for him and him alone. Good thing he wasn't, though.

With a groan, she arched her back, pressing more fully into his palm. "Go on, then," she breathed.

He smacked her through the lacy satin of her red panties. The sound vibrated through the otherwise silent house. So did her answering moan. "Say it. You know what I want to hear," he growled, rubbing the spot he'd just struck.

She shook her head, her hair falling about her shoulders and hiding her face from him. He didn't like that. He wanted to see every emotion as he fucked her senseless. The frustration. The need. The pleasure. He didn't want to miss a thing.

Reaching up, he smoothed her hair gently off her face, and spanked her again. "Say it."

"No," she moaned.

"So stubborn. So sweet." He slipped his hand between her thighs, tracing her slit. "So wet and ready. You know you want me. All you have to do is say those two little words…" He withdrew his hand—which proved to be harder than it should have been—and caressed the other side of her ass. The one he hadn't touched yet. "And you can have me."

She bit down on her lip. He bent down and pressed his mouth to her bare shoulder, kissing her, and pulled back. Without wasting a second, he smacked her ass again. She cried out, trying to squeeze her thighs together, but he inserted his knee between hers so she couldn't. "*Holt*," she moaned, all breathless and sexy.

He smacked her again, harder than before, and rubbed his thumb against her clit, balancing the pleasure with the pain. She cried out, biting her lip even harder. Her stubbornness was fucking hot as hell, but she needed to break before he did. She was testing his strength in ways most women didn't even get close to touching.

He scraped his nail over her clit, biting down on her neck at the same time. She was so hot and ready for him, and damn it, he was ready for her.

"Oh my God," she gasped, dropping her head on the

wall.

"You want more?" he asked, nibbling on her ear as his fingers worked over her. "I can give it to you. Anything you want."

He thrust inside of her, rubbing his palm against her as he did so. Every muscle within him screamed that he needed to take her. Fuck her. Own her.

He didn't do any of those things.

"Don't stop," she said, her voice barely there at all.

"Say it." He stilled, and he pulled his palm away — touching, but not touching where she needed it most. "Say it, damn it," he growled, smacking her ass again.

"Yes, sir!" she cried. "Yes, yes, *yes*."

"Good girl," he said, satisfaction punching him in the chest.

Then he twisted his hand and she cried out, her pussy clenching down tight on him. He brought her to the edge, and then he pulled back, not letting her fall over. Not yet, anyway. Not until he was ready.

Without a word, he ripped his shirt off and tossed it behind them. She looked over her shoulder, her lips parted. "M-May I please turn around?"

He froze with his hands on his buckle. "Why?"

"I want to look at you." She paused. "All of you."

His gut fisted tight. "Yeah. You can look."

She spun slowly, her hands flat against the wall. Nothing prepared him for how hot she'd look, all hot and wanting and *naked*. He'd seen lots of naked women, but none of them affected him like this.

Strange, but true.

Her breasts were full and soft, but the tips were hard.

Begging for his touch. And her waist was narrow, but it flared out generously for her hips. Those hips were meant for a man's hands. *His* hands. And, man, he wanted to touch.

Her scrutiny dipped down, lingering on his abs. She licked her lips and returned his stare. "You should go shirt-less more often. Damn."

Chuckling, he undid his pants. "Thanks."

She reached out and trailed her fingers over his shoulder, tracing the scar from his last tour in Afghanistan. The one where he'd almost died. It was the newest among his marks, scars, and wounds—some visible, some not.

"What happened here?"

He shrugged, his mind closing down. He didn't like thinking about it, and he sure as hell didn't like talking about it. "Nothing. Just an accident."

She looked up at him as if she wanted to say more, but she didn't. Just stared. "I see."

Her fingers dipped lower, skimming over his pecs. She traced another scar, her touch feather light. Funny, how light it was, but yet…it hit him like a punch to the gut.

"I…" He tried to think of something witty to say, but he came up blank. His brain had shut off on him again. How fucking typical. *Asshole.*

She pressed her open palm to his scar. "This another accident that was nothing?"

That one he received when his father had beaten him with a stick for talking back. He hadn't said a word. He'd been ten. "Yeah." He flexed his jaw. "Enough questions. I don't like talking about it."

"Yeah. Okay."

She dropped her hand to his. He still had his fingers on

the button of his pants, but he hadn't undone it yet. Her touch was both erotic and soothing, all at once. So fucking weird. He'd never felt so fucking drawn to one person before. Not like this. "Lydia…"

She dropped to her knees, skimming the hard tips of her breasts over his bare skin as she did so. "Yes, sir?"

"Fuck," he moaned, his abs tensing and jerking at her touch. "I didn't tell you to go down there."

"I know. I'll come back up, if you want me to, though. But I'd rather do this." She undid his button, and he balled his hands at his sides. "May I?"

His breath hitched in his throat, and he wanted to tell her one last time that she should run, save herself from a man like him, because she deserved better. Instead, he fisted his hand in her hair and clenched his jaw. "Yes. Fuck, yes."

She unzipped his pants and tugged them down. He stepped out of them, never releasing his hold on her head. As soon as he was free of the khakis, she closed her hand around his cock through his boxer briefs. "You should walk around without pants, too."

He stiffened, every muscle in his body going harder than the last. "Somehow, I think people might object to that."

"Not women," she said dryly.

He snorted. "Yeah, maybe—" He cut off on a groan. Leaning in, she flicked her tongue over the head of his cock. Even through the cotton of his boxers, it was enough to make him hiss. Enough to get him dangerously close to the edge. And the worst part was? He didn't give a damn.

He wanted to fall.

Chapter Four

Lydia rolled her tongue over him, shutting out the world. She *knew* how to do this, and for the first time that night, she didn't feel like a fish out of the water. Everything else they'd done had been way, way outta her league. Hopefully he hadn't noticed how nervous she was. But in spite of the nerves, she wasn't second-guessing her decision to come home with him. She'd been waiting for a long time for a guy like him to come along. One who made her want...well, *want*.

And with him, she wanted so freaking much.

The way he touched her. Teased her. Caressed her, and yes, spanked her, drove her wild. She had a feeling she could easily become hooked on this. On him.

Good thing she wouldn't get the chance.

Gripping his balls, she tugged his boxers down and closed her mouth over his erection, sucking gently. He groaned and flexed his fingers in her hair, pulling hard enough to bring tears to her eyes. Good ones, not bad. His grip was rough, yet reassuring.

Tight, yet gentle. Perfection.

He groaned. "Lydia, fuck, more."

She took more of him in, moaning deep in her throat. Holt wasn't just large, he was *huge*. Her jaw ached from opening her mouth to accommodate him, but she didn't care. He'd done nothing but blow her mind all night long. Now, it was her turn.

She pulled on his balls, applying what she hoped was the perfect amount of pressure to his sack, as she sucked harder. He groaned and fisted her hair even tighter, yanking it with his movements. "Watching you fuck me with your mouth is so hot."

She lifted her lids and stared up at him. He was even stormier now, all turbulence and passion. His eyes reminded her of the sky on a winter afternoon, right before a blizzard. Deep, dark, and addictive. She could lose herself in him so easily.

"I'll let you go another second, but then you're fucking mine to take. Got it?"

She nodded, sucking even more of him in. He groaned and his arms tightened, flexing in that super sexy way that only men like him could do. His abs jerked, tightening. He didn't have a scrap of ink on him, but he didn't need it. His body was a work of art all on its own. To change it would be a crime to humanity.

She scraped her teeth over the head of his shaft, and he jerked. "Enough. In my room. *Now*."

She let go of him instantly, even though she didn't want to. She knew what came next, and it made her stomach tighten with a mixture of fear and excitement. And need. So much need. As she rose to her feet, he helped her up with a soft touch. "Yes, sir," she said, her heart racing so loudly she barely heard her own words. "Right away, sir."

He cupped her cheek and smiled at her, his gaze tender. But his grip was anything but. Spinning her around, he slammed his body against her back, his hard erection pressing against her butt. He rested his hand across her throat possessively. Not squeezing. Just holding her still. "You're way too good at fucking me with your mouth."

Her stomach clenched tight, doing a flip-flop, and she moaned. She couldn't help it. "Is that a bad thing?"

"Nah." He nibbled on her shoulder. "It's time to get the rest of these clothes off. Follow me."

"Y-Yes, sir."

He led her into his bedroom, never dropping his hold on her. One slow step at a time. "Such a good girl. So obedient."

His hand closed over her breast, and he squeezed it. Desire shot through her, straight to her core. They'd finally entered his bedroom. It was as neat as the rest of the house. It was immaculate. Big bed. One dresser. No pictures. Very impersonal.

Who are you, Holt Cunningham, and what are you hiding from the world?

He led her to the bed, flipped her over, and gently pushed her back until she hit the mattress. Her legs were spread as she fell, and he slipped between them and lowered himself onto her body. The sensation of his skin on hers, with nothing but a few scraps of fabric separating them, was electrifying.

She'd never felt anything like this before.

"You have no idea how crazy you're driving me. I want to fuck you hard, right here, right now. No rules. No foreplay. Just you and me, naked and sweating."

She stiffened beneath him. Because she'd been trying to avoid falling for the wrong guy yet again, she hadn't exactly been climbing in and out of beds throughout college. And after one disastrous, disappointing night with one of the men she'd made an exception for…she hadn't even wanted to. It had been *years* since she'd been in a guy's bed, so she might need a gentler touch than that. "Holt. There's something—"

"Shh." He kissed her, brushing his mouth against hers lightly. "I said I wanted to, not that I would. Do you really think I'd leave you hanging like that? Not make you come? Scream? Beg? Cry for more until I finally gave it to you?"

She moaned when he tugged her hard nipple. "Oh my God."

"Nope, just me." He slid down her body, dropping kisses as he went. "Just you and me."

He bit the skin right above her panty line, making her cry out. Then, without warning, he yanked her panties off and his mouth was on her, making her whole body scream with joy. "Yes. Oh my God, *yes.*"

When his tongue rolled over her, she squeezed his head with her legs, letting out a strangled moan. She'd never felt so…so…*aware.* Every touch, every stroke, drove her higher and higher, until she swore she was floating in the sky. She even saw the stars. His hand slipped under her butt, and he gripped her tight, his fingers digging into her flesh. The mixture of the almost-pain combined with the crazy pleasure sent her flying.

With a cry, she came, her whole body exploding with

pleasure. He let her fall onto the mattress, climbing over her body to open a drawer by his bed. As he took care of business, safety wise, she lay on the bed, blinking up at the ceiling. Holy. Crap. He was amazing. As soon as he had a condom on, he gripped her hips, tilted them up, and slammed his mouth onto hers. She barely had a chance to draw in a breath before he was driving inside of her fully. She stiffened, waiting for her body to adjust to his size.

It took longer than she'd thought it would.

He froze, his mouth still pressed to hers. It was as if someone had hit pause on the DVR, and neither of them could move. And then slowly, oh so freaking slowly, he pulled back and stared at her. "Lydia. Did I…were you…?"

She bit her lip. "No, God, no. I'm not a virgin. It's just been a while. Like…only with one other guy. It was…not good. And it was freshman year in college…so, yeah."

"Jesus." He caught her chin, his touch a little bit rough. "Don't you think you should have fucking told me that? I'd have been slower. More gentle. I wouldn't have…*shit*."

"I'm sorry. I-I can go, if you want."

He reared back. "Not fucking happening." Then he hesitated. "Unless you're regretting…do you *want* to leave?"

"No. Not at all." She bit her lip even harder. "But you seem mad…"

"Not mad. Never mad." He ran his knuckles over her cheek, his eyes tender and no longer stormy blue. Now they were like the soft summer sky on a clear day. "I just feel like an asshole. I should have been gentle. Sweet."

She shook her head. "Don't you dare change a thing you're doing." Tightening her legs on him, she dug her heels into his butt and wiggled her hips experimentally. It didn't hurt anymore, now that her body had remembered what it felt like to have a man inside of her. In fact, it felt pretty darn amazing. "Keep going. It was obviously working for me."

His lips twitched into a smile. "If that's what you want."

Before she could answer, or even form an opinion, he kissed her and moved. And when he moved inside of her... thoughts ceased. Everything did except this. *Them.*

Growling low in his throat, he moved his hips, thrusting in a measured, steady pattern. The slow buildup was a sneaky bastard, creeping up on her when she least expected it. But then it was there, and there was no denying the fact that he was going to kill her. Not *actually* kill her, but *kill* her. He moved his hips faster, his mouth never leaving hers, and cradled her face with both hands. It was amazing how he managed to be both tender and rough, all at once. Were all men like this? Had she been missing out all these years with no lover in her bed? Or was what he had, what *they* had, special?

He broke the kiss off, his lips pressed against her temple. "Fuck, you're going to make me come already. You feel so good...so amazing."

You're telling me? Believe me, I know. She wanted to ask if this was different for him, better, but she bit the words back. Nothing would make her sound more immature than asking *that.* He lifted her hips and thrust into her harder, sending a surge of pleasure rushing through her veins.

"Come for me." He kissed her, resting his mouth on hers as he said, "Let go. I'm here. I have you."

She wrapped her arms around his neck and let go, just as he asked. He moved his hips, and the pressure inside of her built so high it was amazing it didn't rip her in half. Lifting

her hips, she bit down on her lip and strained to grasp onto…
something. Anything. She didn't even know what. But she
needed…

Something sparked inside of her, and it set off a domino
effect. The spark lit a flame of pleasure, and it consumed
her completely. Every nerve within her came alive, and the
pleasure took over.

"Fuck yeah," he groaned, moving inside of her faster.
"So tight. So hot."

He thrust his hips faster, his face red and his expression lost in rapture. It was so sexy, seeing him like this. His
shadowy scruff highlighted the darkness of his eyes until he
closed them. And then he stilled, his entire body tightening
as he came.

With a sigh, he dropped his weight on her, cradling her
close. "Jesus, Lydia. That was…you are…*wow*."

She smiled and buried her face in his shoulder. Yep. A
girl could totally get used to this.

Too easily. Too fast.

Chapter Five

Early the next morning, Holt laid in bed, staring at the ceiling, his arm draped over Lydia. He'd slept like a baby. He didn't remember the last time he'd slept through the night, without nightmares. Without waking up in a cold sweat.

But with her in his arms…he'd done it.

And he'd loved every fucking minute of it, too.

Turning his head, he glanced over at her. The sunlight hit her strawberry blonde hair, making it almost red like her lashes, and her lips were pursed in sleep. She looked even younger like this, and almost angelic. All soft and sweet. He knew better. She *was* soft and sweet—but she had a naughty streak, too. One he'd only just begun to discover.

One he wanted to get to know even better.

He had so many questions for her. Like, what had made her come up to him and say hello, when she'd been so inexperienced in such matters? And what had made her come home with him and give him the best fuck of his life, followed by the best sleep he'd had in years? He didn't know...

But he wanted to find out. And he would.

Because he wasn't ready to let her go yet.

More than anything, he wanted to show her more. Show her how much fun sex could be, since her previous lover had obviously failed in that area. Sex was good. It was fun and freeing. And he wanted to show her *just* how good it could be.

With him.

And if he did that, the feeling he had in the pit of his stomach that he needed more, *lots more*, would go away. It would be the best way to get her out of his system, so to speak. Then when he walked away, he'd know he was good. He'd be done.

They'd both be done.

Her nose scrunched up adorably, and then she rolled over, giving him her back. He stared at the clock, and sighed. It was almost seven, which meant he had to leave for work in an hour. Time to get up and get in the shower. When he got out, he'd wake her up and tell her they should do this a few more times. And if she wasn't on the same page as him?

He'd find a way to change her mind.

Preferably while naked.

Carefully, he extracted his arm from underneath her head and got out of the bed, walking into his bathroom with a grin on his face. For the first time in...well...forever, he had a goal in his life besides work and sleep and living day by day.

He needed to keep her around for a little while longer. Learn what made her tick, and what made her special. Discover why she, out of everyone, made him want *more* than the typical one-night stand from her. There had to be a reason he wanted more.

And once I figure it out, and fix it, I'll run like hell in the opposite direction.

Not yet, though.

He turned on the shower and got in, his mind on her the whole time. And when he shut the water off, his mind was still on her. He made quick work of brushing his teeth and his hair, and came into his bedroom wearing nothing but a towel. Time to wake his sleeping beauty with a kiss.

He walked over to the bed, but when he reached it…it was empty.

He spun in a circle, scanning the floor. The spot where her clothes had been lying in the hallway was as empty as the bed. "Son of a bitch."

She'd pulled a fuck-and-dash on him.

That was usually his play.

Letting out a string of curses, he walked over to the bed, the towel clenched tight in his hands. There was a note on the pillow. Reaching out, he picked it up and scanned it.

Holt,

Thank you for an unforgettable night. It was perfect in every way. Something tells me this morning, if I hung around, would only ruin the perfectness of it all. So…thank you. Again. It was a night to remember forever.

Lydia.

He stared down at her elegant scrawl. She'd run... and left him a thank you note. Un-fucking-believable. She thought her hanging around would ruin things?

Okay. Sure. For most one-night stands, he'd agree, but not with her. She was different. He'd wanted...

It didn't matter what he'd wanted, because she was gone. Whether he'd felt finished or not...*she* was. It was over.

. . .

He walked into the office an hour later, his steps wide and hurried, and irritation at everything in the world eating away at him. Ever since an adorable strawberry blonde had fled his bed, nothing had been going his way. If only he hadn't left her alone...but it was too late. Nothing would change that except a TARDIS.

If he had one of those, he could go back in time. He'd wake her with an orgasm or two, and keep her there until they were *both* finished.

But that wasn't gonna fucking happen.

Jake Forsythe nodded at him as he passed, and he nodded back. Normally he'd stop and shoot the shit, but he was already late, and he had a ton of work to do. Closing his office door behind him, he settled into his chair and opened his browser.

A bunch of files sat on his desk, but he ignored them. He really needed to get started...but the nagging memory of the woman who'd left his house this morning wouldn't shut the fuck up. Maybe if he searched her name, and learned more about her, he'd get over her and move on, like he should have done already.

Let's see...what did he know about Lydia? Well...her name was Lydia. She'd gone to St. Joseph's, and had recently graduated. And she liked *Doctor Who*. Yeah...

That was it.

Fuck me.

He opened Google and typed in *Lydia, St. Joseph's College*. A bunch of results popped up, but it was all shit. After a quick knock, his buddy and coworker, Steven Thomas, came in. He slammed his laptop shut guiltily and glanced up. "H-Hey. What's up?"

"Not much." He sat in the chair opposite Holt's desk. "Shit, man, I had a long night last night."

Yeah, so had he. And the migraine building behind his brows was annoying as fuck. "Why? What happened?"

"I got in a fight with Heather, and she broke it off with me." He ran his hands down his face and sighed. "She said I don't love her enough."

"You don't," Holt said. "You don't love her at all."

"I know." He lowered his hands and stared at Holt. His hazel eyes pierced through him, reminding him of Lydia. "But, honestly, I don't think it's possible to love someone who hates my mother. If they can't get along, then every fucking holiday will be forever ruined."

"There is that," Holt said. He'd never liked Heather. She'd always been standoffish to him. "I'm sorry, man."

"It's fine. I'll be fine." Steven shoved his hands in his pockets. "But now I don't have anyone to bring to that dinner tonight."

"I—" He swallowed hard, the words not coming out right. "Shit, I forgot about that. I'm not even going."

"Is that an option?" Steven asked.

"It is for an IT guy." Holt shrugged and rubbed his forehead. "I don't know about you, though."

"Oh. In that case." Steven grinned. "Want to be my date, man?"

"Hell, no," Holt said, shaking his head for emphasis. The last thing he wanted to do with a migraine coming was socialize with his boss and coworkers. He'd end up coming across as an idiot. "I got out of it, so I'll be damned if I agree to go now. Not even for you."

"Fucker."

"Yep." He leaned back in his chair. "What about Lauren?"

Lauren was Steven's other best friend, who Holt was ninety-nine percent sure was actually his soul mate…if those even existed. They'd never gone there, but it was a ticking time bomb waiting to explode, in Holt's opinion.

They were both just too stubborn to admit it.

"Already tried her." Steven shook his head. "She's got dinner with her latest boyfriend…so that leaves you."

"Ah." Holt shrugged. "Sorry man. Not interested."

"Whatever. Be a dick. I'm out of here. I have to go out to the Branson mansion to watch the old man golf." He dragged his hands down his face. "I'd rather stare at a code all day like you."

"Yeah, well, not everyone can be as awesome as me."

Steven snorted. "If that's what you want to call it. Myself, I'd say 'dorky,' not awesome."

"You can't insult me today." Holt cracked his knuckles and rolled his shoulders. "It's just not possible."

"Why not?" Steven stared at Holt, his hazel eyes latched onto him. "What did you do last night that has you in such a cheery mood? Let me guess. You had another meaningless fuck with some faceless woman who fell for the whole tortured nerdy thing you have going on?"

He cocked a brow. "Tortured nerdy thing? I don't—"

"Yeah, you do. And you make it work." Steven crossed his arms. "Spill it. What did you do last night?"

"Nothing much. Just went to the bar with Gordon, then met someone." He shuffled through the papers on his desk, taking his time to carefully form the thoughts in his head. "And for some reason, I can't stop thinking about her."

Steven sat down. "Seriously? She's actually still on your mind the next morning?"

Holt didn't want to give away too much, since he didn't really know why she was different from the others either, so he shrugged and set the papers back down in the same exact order as before. "What can I say? She was pretty fucking amazing in bed, man."

"Apparently." Steven leaned his elbows on his knees. "Tell me about this paragon of a woman who has you smiling like a fool."

Smiling? Holt froze. He hadn't even realized he'd *been* smiling. He pushed his glasses up into place and shifted his position. "She's got strawberry blonde hair, and does this thing with her tongue and fingers that made me—"

Steven held up a hand. "You know what? Never mind."

"Pussy," Holt teased.

"I jut broke up with my girl, man. I'm not ready to listen to you wax poetic about some redhead yet."

"Strawberry blonde, not red. And when you are ready, I'll be here. I'll even be your wingman."

Steven stood up. "You might not be single for much longer, from the sounds of it."

"The hell I won't be." Holt's phone rang, and he rested his hand on the receiver. "She might be good, but she's not going to hook me like that. I just wanted one more go at her, but she left before I could have one. So she's in the past now...just like the rest of them."

"Famous last words, dude."

Holt flipped Steven off, and the other man left. As soon as the door shut behind him, he picked up the phone. "Holt Cunningham."

"Hey," his boss, Cooper Shillings, said. "Can you come to my office, please?"

"Sure thing."

The line clicked off, and he stood. When the head of Shillings Agency called you down to his office, you didn't waste time. You fucking went. He'd been avoiding him, since he hadn't wanted to stumble over his words in front of the man who could fire him, but he couldn't avoid a direct call like that.

When he got to Cooper's door, he knocked once and heard, "Come in."

Holt walked in. "What can I do for you?"

"I have a new assignment for you."

"Okay." Holt sat down in the chair across from Cooper, who looked at him with bright green eyes. "Where am I going?"

"There's a problem with the system in building five. It's a fucking mess." Cooper dragged his hands down his face and sighed. "I need you to go over there and fix it ASAP, before my dad comes this afternoon. He's been in panic mode over all the technical changes I've made around here, and I don't want to give him more reason to dig his heels in."

Holt stood. "On it."

"Oh, I have a question, too." Cooper said. His brown hair was messy, as if he'd been running his fingers through it all morning long. "Before you go."

"Yeah, boss?"

Cooper shuffled through some papers. "Are you bringing anyone with you to the party tonight?"

"Sir?"

"To the company dinner we're throwing." Cooper cocked his head. "Don't tell me you forgot. I sent out reminder emails last week."

"Of course he didn't forget," Gordon, the man he'd gone drinking with last night, said from behind him. He looked even worse off this morning than he had the last time Holt had seen him. His brown hair was standing on end, just like Cooper's. And he looked like shit—like he hadn't slept at all. "He just wasn't going to go. Said so last night."

"Everyone has to go," Cooper said. "It's a company event."

Gordon pressed his lips together and set a file on Cooper's desk. "So you told me. Don't worry. I'll be there. Here's the VanGuard file."

"Thanks. Since you're at work this morning, I see you didn't leave with the princess after all," Cooper said, frowning.

"Nope. So it'll just be me."

Holt cleared his throat. "I'm not bringing anyone, either."

"Great, I'll let Kayla know."

"Kayla is here, so you don't have to let her know anything," she said from the doorway, her long, wavy hair falling down her back.

Cooper perked up, his shoulders straightening at the entrance of his fiancée. "Hey, babe. What brings you here?"

"Wedding stuff," she said, smiling. "I was looking at dresses down the road, and thought I'd stop in and see how your day was going so far."

"Better now," Cooper said. If possible, he brightened up even more at the mention of their upcoming wedding. Around her, Cooper seemed like a totally different dude. "Did you find the dress?"

"The likelihood of that happening on the first try is one in eight," Kayla said, a soft smile on her face.

Cooper nodded. "So you found it?"

"I totally did." Kayla's face glowed beautifully as she turned his way. "Hi, Holt. Gordon."

"Hi," Holt said, shoving his hands in his pockets.

Gordon cleared his throat, watching the two of them with his fists tight at his sides. For the first time ever, he could sympathize with the feeling. He wasn't sure why, but he could. "I'll leave you guys alone."

"Me, too," Holt said quickly, following Gordon's lead.

"Building five," Cooper called out. As the door shut behind them, Holt heard him say, "Lock the door."

The door lock latched, and Holt looked at Gordon. The other man shrugged back at him. "Don't blame him. If I had someone like her here, I'd lock my fucking door, too. Speaking of which, I heard you met someone last night. Who is she?"

Shit, news travelled fast around here. "No one you'll ever meet."

"Why not?"

"Because I'm not looking for someone who meets my friends." Holt stared him down. "We talked about this last night. Were you listening to me at all?"

"Every word." Gordon shrugged and checked his phone. "But that was before you met her. Sometimes when you meet someone, the right someone, that all changes."

"Uh…" Holt leveled a look on Gordon, the weight of the other man's words sinking to the bottom of his stomach like an anvil for some unknown reason. Gordon's ink seemed to stand out more today, because he was pale. Apparently, this princess of his had really fucked with his head. Another reason Holt didn't want anything to do with love. "Not happening to me. But is that what happened to you and your princess?"

"Yeah, but it doesn't matter. She's gone now."

And with that, Gordon walked off, his shoulders stiff.

That's what love did to a man. It made him miserable. Why anyone would ever willingly put himself through that shit was beyond him. Cooper laughed in his office, and Kayla joined in. *They sound pretty happy to me*, whispered a small voice in the back of his head. Holt ignored it, shrugged, and headed for building five.

He had work to do.

Chapter Six

Lydia tilted her head back and stared at the high ceiling of the ballroom, ignoring, for the moment, the crowd surrounding her. A crystal chandelier hung in the center of the ceiling, but it wasn't actually centered. Whoever had hung it must've been drunk or dizzy, because it was at least two feet too far to the left. It bugged her.

Almost as much as it bugged her to be where she currently was.

Steven had begged for her to come out to eat with him, since his heart had been "broken," and she'd agreed. She'd dressed up, as requested, and met him by her door at six o'clock sharp—only to be told upon arrival that the "dinner" was actually a *work event*. Her initial reaction hadn't just been *no*. It had been a *hell no*. She couldn't risk running into Holt. Not after last night.

But then Steven had gone on to say how he'd broken up with Heather, and Lauren wasn't available. He'd already responded with a plus one, and his buddy Holt wouldn't be there to distract him either, and *he needed her to come so badly*. And since her reason for not going, AKA Holt, wasn't a factor...she'd agreed.

Of course, now she regretted it.

He might not be there, or be planning on coming, but it didn't stop her from staring at the door every time someone came inside wearing a black suit. Or from having a mini-heart attack every time she heard his name. Which was a lot. Too much.

When she looked over her shoulder for the millionth time, Steven sighed. "Relax, Lyd," he said, resting his hand on her upper back. "There's nothing to be so wound up about. You've been to these things before."

Yeah. He had no idea why she was worked up, and he never would. "I'm not wound up. I'm just watching everything and everyone."

"Tell that to the poor sugar packet you mangled."

She glanced down at the pink packet on the table in front of her. He was right. She'd totally butchered it. "It had it coming."

"Oh yeah?" he asked, cocking a brow.

"Shut up, or I'll mangle you next."

Shaking his head, he said, "So mature."

"Yeah, that's me," she muttered.

Steven sighed and took his hand off of her. "You're being awfully antsy, even more so than usual. What's going on in that pretty little red head of yours?"

"My hair isn't red," she said, tossing another destroyed sugar packet into a pile with the first. "It's strawberry blonde."

Steven rolled his eyes. "Yeah. Sure."

"How late is this thing?" She picked up her drink and took a big sip, her heart skipping a beat when someone said Holt's name. No matter how hard she tried not to react, she couldn't help it. "I have a headache."

"Out too late last night?" Steven asked, one brow raised. "What happened, anyway? I heard you and Sam broke up."

"Yeah. We had a differing opinion on who he should sleep with. As in, he felt the need to sleep with other women, and I didn't agree with that decision."

Steven snarled. "That little shit. I'll kill him."

"It's fine." She waved a hand. "I'm over it. It actually happened like three days ago, but I didn't mention it, because I really didn't care."

"Yeah, well, he made a huge mistake. He'll never find another girl like you." He squeezed her hand, then leaned back in his chair and glanced over his shoulder. "And he didn't deserve you, obviously."

Lydia smiled at him. "That's sweet, but according to you…no one does."

"Truth."

She took another sip of wine. "So what happened with Heather, anyway?"

"According to her, I never let her in, and refused to open up to her…whatever the hell that's supposed to mean. Oh, and she didn't think I loved her." He paused, tugging on his bowtie. "I didn't, so she was right about that, at least."

"She didn't deserve you either, then," she said softly.

His grip tightened on his tie. "You've got it wrong. If anything, I didn't deserve her."

Ever since he'd gotten out of the SEALs, Steven had

been different. No big shocker, there, but he used to be so open and free. "Steven…"

"I'm fine. Seriously. We didn't work out, so it's over. That's all." He turned away and finished his drink. "But I wish Holt was here."

She nibbled on her lower lip. "You guys seem awfully close."

"We are." Steven shrugged. "I like him. He's been through a hell of a lot of shit, but he just keeps going. Doesn't let it get him down."

She tapped her fingers on the table. Would it seem weird if she pried for information from him? Or maybe she'd just seem like a curious sister. "What happened to him?"

"He was a sole survivor of an ambush overseas. The IED messed with his head, but he's brilliant. I've never seen anyone code like he does." Steven stared down at his glass. "It takes him longer to form words out of his thoughts now, but he doesn't let it show often. I think that's pretty fucking incredible."

Her heart twisted. So she'd been right yesterday. He'd kept pausing, as if he'd been choosing his words carefully. "Wow. I had no idea."

"Why would you? You've never met him before. Besides, no one really knows. It's not something he wears on a T-shirt." He canted his head. "Why so many questions about him?"

"No reason." Lydia shrugged for extra effect. Time for a change of subject, or he'd start to suspect something was up between her and Holt. "How's Lauren?"

"She's fine. She's got some new sucker on a string, so she's too busy for me," Steven said, his voice tinged with a little bit of jealousy…not that he'd ever admit it. He stood up and tugged on his bowtie again. "I hate these damn things. You want another glass of wine? I'll go get it for you."

"God, yes."

Steven grinned, grabbed their glasses, and headed for the bar. She watched him go, letting the smile slip off her face once he couldn't see her anymore. He seemed sad, which was unusual for him with a breakup. He didn't take relationships seriously.

Never really had.

But as much as she loved her brother, she couldn't remain focused on him for long. Not when a certain glasses-wearing IT guy currently monopolized her thoughts. Her mind inevitably went back to him, and all the things Steven had told her. Knowing he was suffering, *recovering*, made her want to go to his house, knock on his door, and kiss him until he forgot everything. As if *that* would help him at all.

Footsteps came up behind her, and she forced a smile to her face. Steven's voice was louder, which meant he was close, arriving midsentence. "…Introduce you to my date."

The hair on the back of her neck tingled, and she stiffened. Her body had become super aware of something, or someone, and she had a sinking suspicion she knew exactly who that was. But no. It couldn't be. Surely the universe didn't have *that* twisted of a sense of humor.

Behind her, Holt laughed. "I don't know how you found a replacement so fast, but hats off to you, man. Guess you're ready to jump back on that wagon after all, huh?"

The universe did *have a twisted sense of humor.*

This wasn't happening. Couldn't be.

He was here. And he was about to find out who she was, too. Crap, he wasn't supposed to be here. *Why* was he here?

Cursing under her breath, she stood up and headed straight for the door without looking back, her steps hurried and her purse clasped in her hands. If it wouldn't draw too much attention to her, she'd run instead of walk. Seconds from freedom, Steven grabbed her elbow, stopping her in her tracks. "What the hell, Lyd? Why are you running for the door like there's a fire?"

"I, uh...I wasn't running. I was walking." She didn't turn around, in case Holt was behind him watching them. If he didn't see her face, he wouldn't know who she was. She could still manage to escape unseen, if she played her cards right. "Like I said earlier, I have a really bad headache. I'm going to go—"

"There you are. I lost you in the..." Holt's voice trailed off, dying midsentence. "...crowd."

Slowly, oh so slowly, she turned around...knowing what she'd see when she did. Betrayal. Anger. Horror...and regret. Probably a lot of that, once he realized who she was. She didn't want to see that, because she didn't regret a thing.

When they locked gazes, the breath was punched out of her chest. His hollow stare, framed by his glasses, slammed into her like a freaking tidal wave. And he looked devastatingly handsome in a tux and bowtie. It wasn't fair. The smile he'd been wearing faded the second he saw her, and his gaze dipped down to where Steven held onto her elbow. He scowled and flexed his jaw.

"Sorry, man. I was chasing my date down." Steven glanced at her, then released her elbow and rested a hand on her lower back. "She wants to go home now, apparently."

Holt's jaw ticked. "I...we..." He took a breath, his nostrils flaring. "Introduce us first. Please."

"This is Lydia. Lydia, this is Holt. I've told you about him."

Lydia stared back at Holt, frozen in horror, because Holt was staring at her as if she was gum on the bottom of his shoe...or a two-headed snake. "Hi, Holt. Nice to meet you."

"I'm..." Holt pressed his mouth into a tight line and held out his hand. "Yes, nice to meet you, too."

Oh God. She had to touch him. Actually touch him.

In front of her brother.

Reaching out, she slipped her hand into his. The second his fingers touched her skin, her body remembered with very vivid detail what they'd done the night before.

His grip on her tightened, as if he did, too. "How do you two know each other?" he asked.

"She's my sister, man." Steven grinned. "My baby sister, to be exact."

Holt's face paled before flushing bright red. His fingers tightened on hers even more, and his scowl warned of a coming apocalypse. He let go of her, and she missed the touch. "Of...Of course she is. Of course she fucking is."

Steven frowned. "Dude. Language."

"I'm not six, Steven. I occasionally say fuck, too," she said.

She rested a hand on Holt's arm, and he tensed underneath her palm before jerking away. "No, he's right. I'm sorry. Excuse my language. It's nice to finally meet you," Holt said, his voice dripping with fake sugary sweetness. "I've heard so much about you."

She dropped her fist at her side and forced a smile. "Same here. It's nice to meet you."

Steven grinned, seeming completely oblivious to the tension between them. "Two of my favorite people, getting to meet. Maybe tonight won't suck after all."

"Yeah. Imagine that," Holt said dryly.

Lydia stared back at him, accepting as her comeuppance the unspoken words she saw in his stare. He'd want to talk about this some more once they were alone. "Yeah. Imagine it."

Steven glanced at both of them, his brows lowered. "What's wrong?"

"Nothing. Nothing at all," Lydia assured him quickly. She forced a smile before turning back to Holt. "Anyway, like Steven said, I have a headache. I didn't sleep well last night, so I'm going to—"

"Late night?" Holt interrupted, a brow raised.

Her cheeks heated. "Something like that."

"That's what I asked her, too," Steven said, crossing his arms. "Turns out, her dick of an ex-boyfriend broke up with her the other day, so she had a girls night out."

Holt nodded as if he listened intently. "Girls night out, huh? That's the perfect thing to help a girl recover from heartbreak. Or…so I've been told."

"I'm sure it helped her. She has great friends," Steven said.

Her cheeks went hot. "*I* broke up with him, not the other way around. And *she* is right here and can answer for herself."

"Yeah." Holt stared her down. "I can see that."

"I'm going to go now," she said, managing to smile at both of them even though she wanted to scream. "It was lovely to meet you, Holt."

Holt's jaw flexed. "Likewise."

"I'll give you a ride home. Just let me say my goodbyes

to—"

"Steven!" Cooper called out, motioning him over. His fiancée, Kayla, did the same. A pretty brunette woman stood next to Kayla, looking at the three of them. "Come here and meet your new supervisor."

Steven stiffened. "Son of a bitch. I'm too late. Can you wait a little longer, Lyd?"

"I can just get a cab," she said quickly. She could feel Holt's stare burning into her. The sooner she got out of there, the better. "I'll be fine on my—"

Steven glared. "No way. I'm not letting you fight for a cab out there. It's dark, and this isn't exactly the best section of the city."

"I'll be fine. I'm not a child anymore," Lydia said.

"The hell you aren't." Steven fisted his hands. "You're not going home alone, and that's that."

Lydia stiffened. "You listen here, you big oaf. I'll—"

"Now, now. Enough fighting, kids. Cooper's watching, and so is your new boss," Holt said, his voice sardonic. He stepped forward and rested a hand on Lydia's lower back. "I'll take her home and make sure she gets inside safe and sound. You have my word."

Her heart stammered before ramping up to full speed. She couldn't do this. Holt was the reason she was leaving. To be alone with him, in a car, would be dangerous in more ways than one. "N-No. I couldn't ask that of a man I just met. I'll be fine on my own."

"I'm taking you home," Holt said, his voice leaving no room for arguments. "And that's that."

"Yes, sir," she muttered sarcastically.

Holt flexed his jaw, but remained silent.

"Perfect." Steven clapped Holt on the back. "Always the man of the hour, ready to help a guy out."

"Not always," he said under his breath.

The smile on Steven's face slipped for a second, but then it corrected itself. "Thanks, man. And, hey—" Steven glanced at Lydia, and then whispered something in Holt's ear before pulling back. "Got that?"

Holt flexed his jaw. "Yep. Loud and clear."

Without another word, Steven walked over to Cooper, Kayla, and the brunette. Lydia watched him go before turning to Holt. He still had his hand on her lower back. "You don't have to—"

"Oh, but I do." He steered her toward the door. "I really fucking do, *Lyd*."

Her heart hammered away in her ears. "But—"

"You're coming with me, whether you like it or not. So stop fucking arguing and walk."

She wanted to dig her heels in. Refuse. But something told her he wouldn't give in easily. He would make a scene, and her brother would find out about them, and all hell would break loose. So she followed his lead. "What did he say to you?"

Holt steered her out the door. The second they cleared the building, he spun her and pressed her against the brick wall, out of sight of everyone inside, including her brother. "What. The. Fuck?"

"I'm sorry. I didn't—"

"Did you know it was me last night?" Holt's voice was clipped. His glasses reflected the streetlights, but they did nothing to detract from the anger blazing in those eyes of his. "Did you know who I was?"

"Not at first." She licked her lips. "After you said your name, I figured it out, though."

"Son of a bitch. You…I…" His Adam's apple worked as he stared down at her. "Damn it, Lydia."

She swallowed hard. "I'm sorry."

"Why didn't you tell me?" He fisted his hand in her hair. "Why did you let me fuck you like that, knowing you were my friend's baby sister? *Damn* you."

Chapter Seven

Holt glared down at the beautiful woman in his arms—the same one who had haunted his thoughts since she'd left his bed—unable to believe the twisted turn of events. In between his struggles to fix issues in the office and the raging headache he'd had all day long, he hadn't had time to search for her.

Truth be told, it wouldn't have done him any good, anyway.

Never in his life would he have guessed that Lydia was a Thomas—his best friend's little sister. Of *course* he fucking hadn't. Steven talked about his sister all the time, but he rarely used her full name. And even if he had, he'd never in a million years have put two and two together.

He'd been too fascinated with her last night to be logical, damn it.

And his body was being anything but logical now.

Having her there, in his arms, was fucking with his head.

Steven had no idea about the things they'd done last night, and even so he'd felt the need to remind Holt that a best friend's little sister was off limits. As if he needed reminding. He'd already broken the rule. But did it count if you hadn't known at the time she was your best friend's little sister?

Because, God help him, his body still didn't give a damn whose family member she was. He tightened his fist in her hair, his other hand gripping her hip and holding her in place. Touching her only made him want her even more. *Damn it.*

"Answer me," he demanded, feeling even more like a fool than before, which was saying a lot. "Why didn't you tell me the truth?"

"Because I panicked. And after I woke up, I realized if you found out who I was after we…*you know*, it would be awkward for everyone. I mean, you obviously aren't happy with who I am, so why put either one of us through that?" She bit down on her lower lip. "So I left, hoping to save everyone from the whole mess."

The whole mess.

Did that mean she thought he was a mess?

If so, she was right. Most nights, he didn't sleep. Most nights, he drank himself into oblivion after fucking a woman and then sending her on her way with a swat on the ass. Most nights, he hated himself. But last night had been different.

He hadn't sent her away. And he'd slept. Actually fucking *slept.*

Around her, he was a little bit less of a mess, but he couldn't have her. All those thoughts he'd had earlier, of hunting her down and banging her out of his system, should be gone now. The second Steven had introduced her to him she'd become off-limits.

Just as she should have been all along. He wasn't good enough for a girl like her, and he never would be. Steven knew it, and so did he.

"You're…" He cut himself off, trying to think what he wanted to say. She waited patiently. "I-I can't believe this."

"It doesn't have to change anything." She rested her hands on his chest, her touch burning through his shirt. "We had a beautiful night together. It was everything I'd hoped for, and more. Can't we just be happy we had that, and move on? Ignore who I am, and who you are, and just remember the way we made each other feel? Who cares about names, or anything else, really? It was *nothing*."

He tensed. "You're something."

She made a small little sound that he couldn't read. "I was just a one-night stand. Stop trying to give it a different name, or make it into some huge thing it's not. Just let it go."

"But I can't, because you weren't." He lifted his hand and cupped her cheek. "I wanted…I wanted…*more* from you. Another few nights, maybe. For the first time, ever, I wanted more. And now I can't have it."

Blinking up at him, she tilted her head to the side. She looked so fucking cute when she did that. But when she bit down on her lip in the throes of passion?

Hot as fucking hell.

"I want more, too," she admitted.

Every instinct screamed to take her again. After all, she'd just given him the green light. But he didn't fucking move. "We can't."

"Why not?" she asked.

"Because you're off limits." He swallowed hard. "And because you're his little sister."

She rolled her eyes. "Steven probably doesn't even care about that. Don't get me wrong. He hates the men I date, so he'd hate you, too. But it wouldn't be any different from anyone else I've ever brought home."

"Oh, but he does care." He skimmed his thumb over her lower lip, soothing the spot where she'd bitten. "You want to know what he said to me earlier?"

She nodded once, her breath coming fast.

"He said to remember you were his little sister…" He dropped his touch from her, stepping back to safety, pushing his glasses into place. Or, relative safety, anyway. "…And to keep my hands and dirty as fuck thoughts to myself. So, I will."

"He *didn't*."

Shoving his hands into his pockets, he rocked back on his heels. "Oh, but he did."

And I don't blame him one little bit.

"God." She blushed. "That's so…so…"

"Barbaric?" he supplied. "Old fashioned?"

"Yes!" She pointed at him. "Exactly."

"Yeah, well, it is what it is. And I have to respect his wishes."

"Why?" she asked. She slid her hands up his shoulders, slowly and torturously bringing his body to life. "If you want more, and I want more…why not take it?"

He sucked in a deep breath and held it. This was the danger zone. She'd said she wanted more, and damn it, so did he. But not with *her*.

Not with Steven there, watching them.

But even knowing she was forbidden, that she didn't need a fucked up man like him in her life, he wouldn't have the strength to stay away if he knew she wanted him too.

So he did the only thing he could think of to save her from himself. He called out his inner asshole, and had him step up to the plate, bat in hand. "You misunderstood me. I don't want more from you at all. I came to my senses after you left."

She froze. "But you said you want—"

"No, I said I *wanted* more." Closing his hands over hers, he removed them from his shoulders. It was a hell of a lot harder than it should have been. Smirking, he shrugged as if he didn't give a damn about her or anyone. It was a cloak he wore all too well, but tonight it felt wrong. "Past tense. I don't need the trouble sleeping with you again would bring. No offense."

Annnnd home run.

Her cheeks suffused with color, and she took a step back. "Oh. Right."

"Guys like me don't look for more."

She nodded, turning away from him. Even so, he saw the confusion and pain she tried to hide. "I heard you the first time. I *know*."

There was so much he wanted to say. But he didn't.

Instead he tipped his head toward his truck. "My truck's this way. Come on."

She bit her lower lip. "I'm not going with you."

He sighed. "Lydia—"

"No. He thinks you're giving me a ride, so your best friend duty is filled. Believe it or not, I know how to call a cab. I did it at your place this morning."

"We already went over this shit, Lydia." He spread his hand over her lower back, guiding her toward his truck.

He'd been trying to avoid touching her, because touching her made him want her even damn more. She dug her heels into the pavement, but he refused to stop propelling her forward. "Get. In. The. Truck."

"*Fine.*"

Huffing, she followed him, her back tense under his fingers. Funny, he knew the perfect remedy for that. Too bad he couldn't show her. They reached the passenger side door, and he opened it for her. He didn't help her up with a boost on her ass like he had last night. He kept his hands to himself. "In you go."

She climbed in without a word, her silence louder than words could ever be. As he walked around the back of the truck, he dragged a hand through his hair. Then he slid into his seat and slammed the door shut, starting the engine and kicking it into reverse right away.

After he merged onto the road, he tapped his thumbs on the wheel. "Are you still living on campus?"

"No." She crossed her arms and stared out the window. "I'm at Shadyside Apartments."

That was in a suspicious part of town. Not fit for a girl like her. "Steven lets you live there?"

"*Lets?*" Her mouth pressed into a tight, angry line. "No one *lets* me do anything, thank you very much, least of all my brother."

He stopped at the red light and held his hands up. "Fuck, sorry. All I know is my nuts were threatened if I even thought about touching you, so I figured he might be a pain in the ass as far as your living conditions go, too."

"Well, he isn't. And believe it or not, his opinions on who I date don't matter to me, either. If he had it his way, I'd be a nun."

Hell, Holt would, too. Because if he couldn't have her, damn it, neither should anyone else. Logical? Nope. But he didn't give a flying fuck. "I think that the sisterly way of life is highly underrated by modern society. If you were my little sister, I'd—"

She growled under her breath. "Don't even think of going all older brother on me after last night. I will strip naked, right here, right now, to remind you who I am, and what we did. Don't think I won't."

"Oh, believe me. I know exactly who you are." He flexed his fingers on the wheel, his throat tightening on him. The image of her stripping for him was enough to make him forget all about pushing her away. But he had to do it. "And what we did, too."

She glanced out the window, her shoulders stiff. "Whatever."

They fell silent until they reached her complex. As he parked in front of her building, he searched the shadows. Nothing moved. "I'll walk you in safely."

"You don't have to. I'll be fine."

"For the love of—" He broke off, rubbing his throbbing temple. "Jesus, Lydia. Do you have to fight every damn thing I say so fucking hard? I'm just trying to be a good guy, which is nothing less than I should do after what we did. I've made enough mistakes already where you're concerned."

She pressed her lips together and gripped the door handle. "Last night was nothing. People have one-night stands all the time. Especially *you*."

With that, she opened the door, hopped down, and stormed off for the entrance. A headache was building behind his forehead, and he knew D-Day grew closer. Soon, he'd be in bed, incapacitated and useless. "Son of a fucking bitch," he mumbled under his breath, opening his own door and going after her. "Wait just a second."

"No," she called over her shoulder. "Go *home*, Holt."

He hurried his steps and easily caught up with her right outside her door. Reaching out, he grabbed her elbow. "Who told you that I had lots of one night stands? Steven?"

"You said it last night, several times. And even if you hadn't, you wouldn't need to." She gestured toward him. "You've got the whole thing down to a science."

"And what the hell is that supposed to mean?"

"You know exactly what it means," she snapped, pulling free. "You bring girls home with you all the time, tell them how it's one night only, and not to get attached. And I'm just another one of them, so stop making me into this horrible thing you did wrong in your life, and making me feel even worse than I already do."

"Lydia, I—"

She held her hands up. "Look, I get it, okay? You regret touching me, and you don't want to ever see me again. I was a mistake. A huge one. So move on, forget all about me, and go home. We don't have to ever set eyes on one another again."

"Wait, I didn't say that." He shook his head, struggling to answer her. "It's just...I...fuck." Damn it, the words wouldn't *come*.

"Yeah, you did. I think you said it at least a million times, in a million different ways." She opened the door and walked inside. "Goodbye, Holt. It's been real. You'll never have to see me again, or remember the night you stooped so low that you actually screwed a girl like me."

He should let her walk away. He should leave with empty hands and an even emptier heart. But he couldn't. Not with her. Not now. He wasn't supposed to want her, wasn't supposed to go after her, but damn it, he did want her. He really fucking did.

What was even worse than the fact that he should be resisting temptation—and *wasn't*—was the fact that she wasn't even giving him a chance to form a reply.

And that pissed him off even more than his slow brain, or his inability to keep his hands to his fucking self. He followed her inside, his blood pumping. He didn't bother with trying to put his thoughts into words. Not this time. Instead, he caught her, tossed her up against the wall, growled...and kissed her.

And, God help her, she kissed him back.

Chapter Eight

Lydia collapsed against the hard wall, clinging to his even harder chest. She didn't know what the heck was going on in his brain right now, but she knew one thing. All she'd been able to think about since last night had been kissing him. If he wanted to do it again, right here in her hallway, then so be it.

She'd kiss him back.

He pressed closer and ran his hands over her body, squeezing her breasts and rolling his thumbs over her nipples. She moaned into his mouth, needing more. Needing him. He broke the kiss off, resting his forehead on hers and letting out a shattered breath. "Jesus, Lyd. You have no idea how fucking hard it is for me not to take you right here. Right now."

She moaned. "Then *do* it. What's stopping you?"

"Nothing. Everything." He nipped at the sensitive skin over her pulse, and then kissed away the sting. At the same time, he slipped his hand up her dress and cupped her core, pressing his palm against her where she needed him most. "But I had a taste of that tight pussy of yours, and I want more. So much more."

She moaned again. She couldn't help it. "So take it, damn it. Take me."

"Roommate?"

"Out of town." She undid his jacket. "Won't be back till next week."

He kissed her again, shrugging out of it as he did so. The sooner they got naked, the better. By the time he had the door kicked closed behind them, she was on the last button of his white button up shirt. She slid it over his arms and it hit the floor. He lifted her against him, his mouth never leaving hers, and she wrapped her legs around his waist securely.

He cupped her butt with his big hands and walked toward the bedroom, his tongue gliding over hers. Digging her heels into his upper back, she ran her hands over his chest. He was so hard and smooth. So irresistible. He paused in front of her door. "Yours?"

She nodded and kissed him again. Growling, he opened the door and barged into her room. Within seconds, she was on the bed, and he was on top of her. His hand slipped up her inner thigh, teasing her with almost-there touches.

Then the *almost* touching was gone, and he had a hand inside her thong. When he thrust a finger inside of her, she cried out and arched her back. "Yes."

"Shit, you're so fucking tight." He pulled back just enough to make her scared he might be pulling away completely, but then he thrust two fingers inside of her. "And so fucking *mine*."

She nodded frantically. "Yes, God, I need—"

"I know what you need, Lyd." He twisted his fingers, and she cried out. "You need *me*."

The pleasure was already building. Intense. Fierce. Inescapable. "Yes. Oh my God, *yes*."

Slamming his mouth down on hers again, he moved his fingers over her even faster. She was so close. One more twist of his fingers, and she'd be—

An old-school ringtone sounded, and a phone vibrated against her leg. Holt froze, both on top of her and inside of her. And just like that, the reality of what they'd been about to do hit him. She could *see* it in his face. He swallowed hard, his fingers still deep inside of her. "Shit. I…we…"

"Holt." She framed his face with her hands, forcing him to look at her. "It's fine. You don't have to stop."

"Yes. Yes, I do." He slid off of her, taking his magical fingers with him. "Damn it, Lydia. You never should have let me inside. You never should have…I never…"

Frustration balled up in her stomach, making her sick. Sitting up, she smoothed her dress over her thighs with a trembling hand. "Get out. Now."

He ran his hands down his face and took a minute to compose his words. "Look, this has nothing to do with you."

"Oh, I know that." She lifted her chin, staring him down. "But I'm pissed anyway. You can't do this. Come in, kiss me, and then act as if I'm the worst mistake you've ever made."

He watched her over his fingers. "Lydia…"

"No. Don't." Shoving his shoulders, she snapped, "Just *go*."

Still, he hesitated. He took in every detail of her body, and for a second she thought he was going to come back to her. But he stood his ground. "You deserve more than I can give you. You deserve a prince, not a broken man like me. We will never, *ever*, live in a world where a guy like me can treat a girl like you the right way."

Refusing to reply to that, she pressed her lips together.

"It's true. You can ignore me all you want, but it's true." He stared down at her, his bare chest heaving. "I've seen things...done things...that no one should have done or seen. And now I'm falling apart. I'm no good for you. For anyone. Stop letting me in. Stop kissing me. Stop listening to anything I say. Just *stop*."

And with that, he turned on his heel and left. She watched him go, her heart wrenching. Even though she couldn't tell if she was more angry or upset, she knew one thing. He thought he didn't deserve her. Thought he was somehow lacking something. He was wrong. She almost chased after him. Almost tried to get him to see himself the way she did, but she forced herself to stay still. Nothing she did, or said, would change the real issue at hand. She was his best friend's little sister...

And he didn't want her.

• • •

The next morning Lydia sat in her living room, her phone in front of her next to her open MacAir. She'd typed in two little words on the Google search bar, but she hadn't hit return yet. She glared down at the computer, her heart accelerating at just the appearance of his name on her screen. *Holt Cunningham.*

She could hit the button. Read all about his past, so she

could find a way to make him see she wasn't scared of him. He seemed to think he was some kind of monster, but he was wrong. He was a damaged man, sure. But that didn't make him a *bad* one.

Did it?

Just as she was about to hit search, a knock sounded at her door. She stared at it. It wasn't even seven o'clock yet. Who would be here this early? Slowly, she walked to the door and plastered her face against it. Through the peephole, she saw...

Oh, crap.

Gasping, she smoothed her hands over her hair. It was probably a frizzy mess, but that wasn't a huge surprise since she'd spent the night tossing and turning. *Great. He looks like a model, while I look like a troll.* Not much to do about it now.

Not if she wanted to let him in—and she did.

After taking a deep breath, she cracked the door open. "What are you doing here?"

He held out a bouquet of flowers. "I wanted to give you these. I saw them on my way to work, and the green ones looked like your eyes..." He broke off, his cheeks red. "I mean... I thought of you..."

They looked like my eyes? *God, he's trying to kill me.*

Her heart did a flip-flop and then soared. Opening the door more, she took the blooms and brought them to her nose. They smelled lovely. "You bought me flowers?"

"Yeah." He cleared his throat and shoved his hands into his pockets. "I did."

"Why?"

"I don't know," he admitted. "I saw them, and I thought

of you, so I bought them."

She stared at him, and he stared right back.

Neither one of them spoke.

After a while, he shifted on his feet. His gray pants hugged his body way too freaking closely, and he wore a button up blue shirt. His glasses were perched on his nose, and his hair was styled to the side. He looked hot as hell, of course. He always did. "I'm sorry for last night. For what I did."

"For touching me, or for stopping?" she asked, gripping the doorknob.

"Both." He shifted on his feet. "I shouldn't have done either one."

She nodded. "Because I'm Steven's little sister."

"Yes." He shrugged. "I'm not going to lie and say I don't want you. I do. But I just got out of hell, and I'm trying to be an honorable man. Trying to do things right. To get my head on straight. Starting something with you now…it wouldn't be right. So I can't."

She got that. Steven was still a mess, and he'd been home a lot longer than Holt. He hadn't been injured as badly as him, either. If Holt didn't think he was stable enough to be with her, even temporarily, then she wouldn't push him.

Swallowing hard, she nodded once. "Okay. Apology accepted."

He took his hands out and rubbed his jaw. "I like you, Lydia. I know we met and jumped right into bed, and then there was last night…"

"Yeah, there was last night." She tightened her fingers on the stems, knowing what was coming next. She might as well beat him to the punch, and say it first. "You want to forget that ever happened, and be friends? Platonic friends."

He nodded. "Yes, exactly. Well, not forget, necessarily. But not do it again."

"Yeah. Sure." Her heart twisted. "It was just a one-night stand. No reason to dwell on it. Right?"

Something flashed across his face for an instant, but then it was gone. "Right. We can't do it again, but that doesn't mean I regret you, or what we did. Or that I don't want to see you again. I've never really been friends with girls, but I want to be yours."

"I see." She gave him a tight smile. "All right, then."

"Good." He stared at her some more before clearing his throat. "The wounds on my chest? They came from war. I was injured in battle, right before I came home."

She blinked at him. She'd asked him about them the night they'd first met, and he'd blown her off. She knew telling her now was a way of showing her he was serious. That he wanted them to share. That he actually wanted to be friends. "I'm so sorry for that."

He nodded. "We're good?"

"We're good," she said softly.

He glanced over his shoulder, tugging on the hair at the back of his head. "All right. I better go to work, then."

"Yeah, or you'll be late." She forced a smile and stepped back into her apartment, the flowers still in her hands. "Thanks for stopping by, and for the flowers."

"Anytime."

He stared at her for another second, his silence saying so much and yet not enough, then turned and left. She watched him go, her heart pumping loudly.

He'd brought her flowers. So they could be friends.

Unfortunately for him, that only made her want him more.

Sighing, she closed her door and walked into her apartment, the flowers pressed to her nose as she inhaled their scent. Another knock sounded, and she started for the door. Without looking through the peephole, she set the bouquet down and opened the door. "Did you forget—?"

She broke off, because it wasn't Holt. It was Sam, her cheating ex. "Hey, babe."

"Uh...hi." She tightened her grip on the doorknob. "What are you doing here?"

"I forgot some things and wanted to grab them."

"Okay..." She stepped back and let him inside. "What did you forget?"

"You."

She blinked. "What do—?"

"I'm sorry. I never should have slept with Joan."

"Yeah, well, you did." She stepped aside, motioning out to the hallway. "Now get out before I—"

"I miss you, babe."

He wrapped a hand around her waist and pulled her into his arms. She barely had time to register what was happening before his mouth was on hers. Unlike last night, when Holt had done the same thing, her reaction was nonexistent—unless you counted repulsion. Slipping her hands in between them, she shoved him back, but he didn't budge. Twisting, she managed to free her mouth from his. "Sam, *stop it*."

"Why?" He backed her against the wall, not letting go. He crushed her between the wall and his chest, and instead of fearing him, she wanted to scratch his eyes out. "I saw that asshole leave your building just now. And then I figured out why we didn't work. I wasn't enough of a jerk for you. I didn't press you for sex, or anything."

She shoved at his shoulders again. "Neither did he, dumbass. I just gave it to him willingly."

"Well, now you can give it to me, too," he said angrily.

Her stomach turned. "Over my dead body."

"So melodramatic." He laughed cruelly. "Then again, you always were. I don't know how I didn't notice it before. But before I go, let me show you how a real man—"

One second he was there. The next, he was gone. She blinked and then tugged her shirt down. It had ridden up in her struggle. But who had—?

Holt slammed Sam against the door, his face red. Sam held his hands up, looking like the scared little boy he was. "Look, man, I wasn't—"

"Yes, you were, *man*," Holt growled, his grip on Sam's throat flexing. "Give me one fucking reason not to kill you right here, right now."

Sam paled even more. "Dude, I-I-I didn't—"

"Not good enough."

"You can't kill me over a kiss," Sam cried. "It was just a kiss!"

"Again, not enough." Holt twisted his mouth. "I've killed for a hell of a lot less. Believe me, I won't give a damn when I do it to you."

Holy crap. He hauled his fist back, seeming fully intent on punching Sam in the face. He'd been a jerk, yes, but she wasn't about to watch Holt beat the life out of him for it, thank you very much. "Holt."

One word. One simple word.

But it seemed to stop him in his tracks.

"Lydia," he replied, his fingers flexing.

"Don't hit him." She walked up, heart racing, and rested a hand on his back. "He's not worth it. Trust me on this."

His fingers flexed. "You're right. He's not. But you are."

"Holt…" She wasn't sure what to say to that. He said so many sweet things, but then he pushed her away every time she got too close. "Let him go."

Holt stared at him, looking deadly and dangerous. "No."

"Look, man, I'm sorry." Sam licked his lips, not daring to so much as blink. "I'm sorry."

"Say it to her, not me."

Sam glanced at Lydia for all of two seconds before slamming his attention back to Holt. She didn't blame him. Holt pissed off was a sight to behold. "Sorry, Lydia."

Lydia crossed her arms. "Just go—"

"Now tell her it won't happen again, and that you'll never come near her." Holt pressed on his throat and grinned. "Because if you do, I'll kill you. I swear I won't let her stop me next time."

Sam nodded frantically. "I'll stay away."

"Good." Holt shoved him one last time, then stepped back. "Now get the fuck out of here before I change my mind."

Sam ran. Legit ran.

She didn't blame him one little bit.

As soon as he was gone, Holt slammed the door shut behind him and locked it. He ran his hand through his hair, his back still to Lydia, and let out a long breath. When he turned, the murderous glow was gone. But he still looked ready to pounce.

"Are you okay?"

She nodded. "I'm f-fine."

"I saw him come in as I left, but it took me a second to recognize him. Once I did, I came back up to make sure you were okay." He swallowed. "I'm sorry I wasn't faster."

She licked her lips. "But... Thank you."

"Why did you—?" He broke off, squaring his jaw. Lydia gave him time to think. "Why did you let him in?"

"He said he needed to pick up some stuff here. I hadn't seen anything of his, but I figured maybe I'd missed it." She shrugged, swallowing hard. "So I let him in."

"Lydia, don't let guys like him in." He caught her chin, his touch feather light. "As a matter of fact, you shouldn't let guys like me in, either. I'm starting to think this whole nun idea of Steven's is a good one."

She tried to laugh at his joke—at least, she *thought* it was a joke—but she choked on it, and all that came out was a weird sobbing sound. She covered her mouth and wanted to run for her room, crawl into bed, and never come out again. It wasn't that she was scared or anything. There was no doubt in her mind that she would have stopped Sam before she'd let him actually hurt her. She just felt...

Icky. Dirty.

As if she needed a shower.

Holt paled, took a step toward her, but stopped. "Lydia."

"I'm fine." She held her hand up, the other still covering her mouth. "Really."

He took another step, cursed under his breath, then closed the distance between them. Within seconds, he had her in his arms and was walking toward the couch. As he sat down with her and kissed her temple, he gently ran his fingers through her hair. "Shh, it's okay. Don't be scared."

"I-I'm not."

"Yes, you are. I should have fucking killed him," he growled. "Next time, let me."

"No. And like I said, I'm not scared." She lifted her hand to touch his face. At the last second, she remembered she wasn't supposed to be intimate with him, so she let her hand fall to her lap…empty. "I'm pissed off."

His lips twitched. "I am, too."

"He's such a douchebag. To do that. To kiss me like that…" She shuddered and fought the urge to swipe her hand across her mouth again. "What a…a…"

"Fucking prick," Holt supplied. "Loser. Asshole. Scum of the fucking earth."

"Yes, all of those," she said, nodding. "And more that I can't think of right now because I'm all worked up."

He cupped her cheek, his touch tender. Apparently the rules didn't stop *him* from touching her all he wanted. "We can write them all down so you remember for next time."

"There better not *be* a next time. I never want to see him again."

"You won't." His jaw flexed. "Not if I have anything to say about that."

Her stomach twisted hard to the left, and it was then that she realized she was cradled in his lap, and he was holding her close. Close enough that she could feel his erection pressing against her butt, and smell the manly scent of his cologne. Close enough that they both froze, breaths held, as they became aware of one another.

It made her want to forget all about his words. Forget all about being *friends*. She had enough friends, damn it. She desired *him*. But he didn't want her. And she had to respect that. Had to respect *him*. So, she cleared her throat and wiggled free. As she slipped off his lap, he let out a small groan. She hadn't meant to rub her butt up against his erection… but she totally had.

"Jesus, Lydia."

Her cheeks heated. "Sorry. So sorry. Uh, thanks for the rescue, by the way. You're a good friend to have around."

"Any time, Lydia." He stood up awkwardly, tugging on his khakis. "Any fucking time."

Leaning down, he cupped the back of her head and kissed her temple. When he pulled back, his lips hovered over hers. So close, and yet so freaking far. "I have to go to work now, but don't open the door for any strange men. Especially me."

She swallowed hard. "I'll always open the door for you. If you don't want me to let you in, then don't knock."

His fingers tightened on her hair. "I wish it was that easy. I really fucking do."

With that, he let go of her and left without another word. The second the door closed behind him, she collapsed against the couch, her fingers pressed to her lips.

What did that even *mean*?

Chapter Nine

On Monday morning, Holt glanced at the clock for what had to be the millionth fucking time. All day long, Lydia had been on his mind. Her smell. Her laugh. The way she'd clung to him, all fiery and pissed off at her douchebag of an ex. But mostly, he'd been thinking about how close he'd been to fucking her the other night, and how he never should have stopped.

Sure, she deserved better. But in his opinion, most women deserved better than the men they were with. It was always that way, because men were dicks by nature. Maybe it went against his DNA to admit that, but what the fuck ever. It was true. So, yeah, he was a dick.

But so was every other guy out there.

If she had to be with one of them—if she refused to be sensible and join a convent—why couldn't it be him?

A knock sounded on the door, and he glanced up gratefully. Today had to be the longest day in the history of all mankind, so he'd welcome the distraction. Any distraction. "Come in," he called out.

Cooper Shillings popped his head in, scanned the room, and walked inside. "Hey, man."

"Hello." Holt sat up straight and tugged on his shirt. He'd been slouching, damn it. His boss rarely came into his office, so he hadn't expected him to do so today. "How can I help you?"

"Have you talked to Gordon lately?"

Holt blinked. "Yeah, Friday. Why?"

"I want to do something for him, because of that whole princess thing." Cooper waved a hand, his green eyes brighter than normal, and sat in front of Holt's desk. "Apparently, when I fell in love with Kayla, I became a fucking softie and want everyone else to be happy, too."

Holt choked on a laugh. "Okay. What do you want me to do?"

"He's listed as private and is unsearchable in the databases, so I want to send his address to the queen. Just in case." Cooper paused, then pulled a file out of his lap. "This is her information. Just see that she finds it in her phone, or on her laptop somehow. But he can't know we did it. Neither can she."

Holt blinked. "Let me get this straight. You want me to hack a queen's phone, give her Gordon's number, and then back out of it and act like I never did it?"

Cooper nodded once. "Yep. Exactly."

Exactly the distraction he needed. "Perfect." Holt grinned. "I'm on it."

"Thanks, man." Cooper stood and tugged on his suit jacket. "It means a lot to me, and him, even if you'll never get the credit."

"I—" He shrugged, taking a second to gather his thoughts because an intense pain in his head cut off his train of thought. "I don't need any credit."

"Good." Cooper hesitated, running his hand through his light brown hair. "How have you been since starting here? Adjusting okay to civilian life?"

Holt glanced up. *Hell no.* "Uh…"

"I know your story. It's the story we all have." Cooper shrugged. "But yours is a little worse. I know it's been tough for you to adjust to the changes you've been forced to accept."

What all did he know? Holt certainly hadn't told him shit. "My struggles are no different than anyone else's."

"Yeah, that's true, I guess." Cooper eyed Holt. "I saw on your physical report that you were having a few symptoms from the IED attack. Do you still suffer from headaches? Or episodes where you can't think properly?"

Like being unable to form a quick-witted reply? Like being able to sleep, or feel normal? Like never forgetting what it was like to shoot his squad leader in the head, after he'd begged him to put him out of his misery? Of course he still had issues with all of that shit, but if he admitted it… Cooper would sack him. He would have to.

More than ever, he missed that life he'd once had before that horrible night in the fucking desert. Missed the guy he used to be. Missed being normal. *But you felt normal with Lydia, and you slept, too*, an inner voice whispered. *You could have it, with her.*

"Holt?" Cooper asked, his brows lowered. "You in there?"

How long had he been lost in thought?

He cleared his throat. "Uh, yeah, sorry. It's been a tough road, but I'm fine. I don't have any episodes any more. The headaches are gone, too. Thanks for giving me the job. I know there had to have been more qualified applicants."

Ones who could still function fully. One who didn't have a fucked up brain that couldn't form coherent thoughts half the time. Who didn't deserve to be fired for lying through his teeth to his boss. But Holt didn't have a choice.

What boss in their right mind would keep a guy who suffered from migraines so severe he couldn't function at a hundred percent for a whole week?

"I only hire the best," Cooper said, not dropping his stare. "I hired you because you were the man for the job. End of story."

Holt swallowed hard. He didn't feel like the best man for anything. Not even for himself, and certainly not for Lydia. "Thanks."

"Sure." Cooper inclined his head toward the file. "Let me know when it's done, okay?"

"Absolutely."

The door closed behind Cooper, and Holt leaned back in his chair, his fingers linked in front of his stomach. He liked his boss. In fact, he liked all the people he worked with. They were all fighters, like him, with various amounts of damage. Both inside and out. Of course, when he was with them, he felt like even more of a fuck up.

At least they didn't stumble over words, or stay up all night staring at the unmoving ceiling fan because when it was on, they had episodes. Flashbacks of helicopters, and bombs, and blood. So much fucking blood. It felt like no matter how many times he showered, he'd never wash it all away.

Hell, Cooper was engaged and happy as hell. Jake was in love with a woman who hated him, but at least he'd been strong enough to fall in love in the first place. And Gordon was together enough to get a fucking *princess* to fall in love with him. They just needed a little push to get them back together, and it was Holt's job to give it to them.

Again, Lydia's laugh crossed his mind, taunting him with its clarity. With its perfection. After he'd left her high and dry the other night, he'd had nothing but his hand and his memories of her to keep him company. And that's all he'd had since, too. After easing the need a little bit, he'd felt as if he had a good hold on what to do next.

His best friend was her brother, so he obviously couldn't avoid her forever—even though he'd done a pretty good job of it up until now. On top of that, he liked her. He didn't want to avoid her. So at two in the morning he'd come up with the brilliant idea to be her friend. Her fucking *friend*.

Shit, he'd have better luck flying with bird wings than remaining her friend.

He'd sworn to himself he wouldn't touch her again, and he'd lasted, what, ten minutes? They hadn't even made it inside the building before he'd been on her, his hand between her legs and his tongue in her mouth.

But he was going to be her *friend* now? Dumbass.

Shaking his head, he opened the file and set to work at giving Gordon a shot at his happily ever after. A happily ever after he'd never have for himself.

By the time he was finished, it was ten after five, and he was free to go home. Still, he sat there at his desk, staring ahead. It was Monday night. Would Lydia be going out with friends? Hitting up a bar? Hitting on some guy? He'd introduced her to how much fun sex could be, so who was to say she wouldn't want more now?

From some other guy, who might not treat her right?

He rose and grabbed his jacket. He needed a stiff drink or ten. He also needed to find some nameless girl, with an unmemorable face, bring her home, and fuck her until he forgot all about Lydia, and her beautiful laugh. Until he forgot how much he wanted her.

And how much he couldn't have her.

• • •

Lydia leaned closer to her friend, struggling to hear her over the loud music. After her craptastic day, she'd agreed to go out dancing and drinking in a local bar. But now that she was here, she wished she hadn't. Who the heck went to bars on a Monday night? She'd prefer to be at home in her *Doctor Who* robe, reading a good book, or binge watching some of her favorite episodes with David Tennant in them.

But instead, she was in a bar, in a too short skirt, in a too tight top, wearing a pair of heels that would more likely than not have her flat on her butt by the end of the night.

On top of that, she had no idea what to do about the phone call she'd gotten earlier. She'd been offered a job in Delaware. One that was amazing, and perfect, and a once-in-a-lifetime opportunity. But it was in Delaware.

She didn't *want* to move to Delaware.

"Hey," Gianna pointed over her shoulder, "that hot guy over there wants you to dance with him."

Lydia looked. Sure enough, a brown haired man watched

her. As soon as they made eye contact, he smiled and held up his drink. "Want one?" he mouthed.

He was attractive enough, if you were into that totally-hot-in-a-movie-star way type of guy. Which every woman in America was. But for some reason…she didn't want to go over there. Didn't want a drink from him. "He's cute," she said noncommittally.

"Cute?" Gianna rolled her eyes. "He's beyond cute. He's perfect. Go over there."

"But—"

"We're not here to ignore cute boys. We're supposed to be having fun. Forgetting all about responsibilities and job offers. So stop thinking." She pushed Lydia forward. "And *go*."

Lydia stumbled forward, glaring over her shoulder at her friend as she went. When she reached the guy's side, she smiled at him. He was even cuter up close, but his eyes weren't right. And his hair was too light. And he didn't have glasses on.

"Whatcha drinking, baby?" the guy asked.

She flinched. That's what Holt had called her that night she'd gone home with him. At the time, it had seemed hot. But from this guy, it felt lazy. "Cranberry vodka, please."

He turned to the bartender and ordered the drinks. As he did so, she scanned the crowd for Gianna. She was off chatting to some guy Lydia didn't recognize. Just as she started to sweep her gaze back toward her drink partner… she saw *him*. Holt sat four seats down, next to some blonde chick who easily could have been Barbie.

And from what Lydia could see, Barbie was way too ready to go home with him. Every time he said something, she tossed her head back and laughed hysterically.

No one was *that* funny. Not even Holt.

He watched the other woman, his lids lowered and his expression bored. He looked as if he'd rather be anywhere but here. Or maybe that was what she was feeling, or wishful thinking. Because seeing him flirt with some bimbo was definitely high on her list of things she didn't want to do. Or see.

"Here you go," the guy next to her said.

She forced herself to look away from Holt, whose attention had dipped even lower on Barbie's body, and smiled at the guy. Suddenly, it seemed highly important that she give this guy a fair shot at being cool. "Thanks. What's your name?"

"Paul," he said, his focus securely locked on her boobs. "Yours?"

"Lydia. What do you do, Paul?"

He pressed his lips together. "I'm in between jobs right now, but I'm in marketing."

"Oh, cool." She took a sip of her drink, and without permission, her eyes peeked at Holt. He'd spotted her, and was glaring at her over Barbie's head. She looked away quickly, her heart racing. "Uh…"

She couldn't think of a darn thing to say to this guy.

He didn't seem to mind. After tossing back his whiskey, he swiped a hand over his mouth and smiled. "Want to dance?"

She squinted at Holt again. He leaned into Barbie, and spoke slowly into her ear. Barbie shivered and rested a hand on Holt's thigh. Lydia was two seconds from storming over there and forcibly removing it, but then she remembered that he didn't want her to be his. She hadn't even seen him since he'd told her he wanted to be her friend, saved her from Sam, and then left. So he was free to do what he pleased.

And so was she.

"Absolutely." She downed her drink way too fast, then stood on her feet. The room spun, but she didn't care. She needed to do something to take her mind off of Holt and all the things that came with him. He'd obviously done the same to her. "Let's go."

Paul grabbed her hand and brought her out on the floor. The second he found an empty spot he was on her. He danced, but his hands roamed places they didn't need to. Nothing crazy or improper, but close enough to make her tenser than she should have been. Maybe it was because of the earlier encounter with Sam, or maybe it was because somewhere behind her, Holt was hitting on Barbie…but for some reason, she wasn't feeling it.

Determined to stick it out through the dance, she matched the guy's moves. He was actually a pretty good dancer. And by the time they'd finished the first song, she'd changed her mind about leaving. She was actually having fun, and she hadn't had fun in way too long. But she wouldn't be going home with the guy. He was a distraction from real life, and nothing more.

The next song cued, and she grinned at Paul. "This is fun," she shouted.

"Yeah, it is!" he shouted back, slipping his hands behind her back. "You're a good dancer."

His fingers rested right over her butt, but didn't touch. He kept it PG-13. And, really, once she was over the disappointment of him not being Holt, he seemed like a pretty cool guy. Too bad his touch didn't light her on fire like Holt's. Leaning in, she replied, "Thank you. I—"

"Excuse me," said a voice she knew better than her own. "May I cut in?"

Paul looked at her, his face full of disappointment. It was on the tip of her tongue to say no. To send Holt away. But that wasn't going to happen. "Can you give us a minute, please?" she asked Paul.

He nodded once, his eyes on Holt. "Sure thing."

After he left, she crossed her arms. "What's up?"

"We're on the dance floor, so we should probably dance," he said, dipping his head down so he could speak in her ear without shouting. "Dance with me, Lyd?"

Her heart twisted at the soft question. The way he used her nickname never failed to make her quiver, which was silly, really. It was just a name. "Sure."

They started moving to the music, which was an admittedly slower beat than the song before it. His hips moved in a way that she didn't think was possible, and he kept his hand on her lower back the whole time. His touch burned through her thin shirt. If she didn't know better, she would swear she wasn't wearing one at all, from how distinctly she felt him. *Knock it off, Lydia. He's not interested.*

"Why did you come over here?" she asked, trying to distract herself from the man, who was driving her insane without even trying. "Isn't Barbie going to miss you?"

He cocked a brow. "Is that her name? I didn't ask."

"Do you always flirt with people without asking their names?"

"All the time." He shrugged. "Most of the time, I never plan on seeing them again…come morning. Except with you."

For some reason, knowing he had a protocol made her sick to her stomach. "Sorry for ruining your thing. Though, you don't *have* to see me if you don't want."

He rolled his hips in a way that screamed sex. Dirty, dirty

sex. "We're in the same bar, so I kind of did have to see you."

"Not really." She swayed, and he stared at her hips. When he glanced back up, he wore a naughty smirk. The same one that had pulled her under his spell the other night. "You could have kept talking to Barbie, and I could have kept dancing with Paul, and this wouldn't be happening."

"Ah, but it's not that easy." He led her toward an alcove, never breaking beat once. "I saw you, and then I saw him, and I had to step in."

Her heart fluttered. "Why?"

"Isn't that what friends do?" He tugged her into the shadowed hall, the darkness enveloping them both. She stood still, her hands fisted at her sides, as he circled her, like a shark with its prey. She swore she felt his fingers brush her hip, but it might have been her imagination. "Stop friends from making mistakes?"

"Yeah." Her nails dug into her palms. "But who says he was a mistake?"

"Did he call you 'baby'?"

She blinked. "Well, yes. But so did you."

"When I wanted to fuck you and forget you, I did. That's what he wanted. I haven't called you baby since I realized who you were. Since I realized…"

She cocked her head. "Since you realized what?"

"It doesn't matter. He's no good for you."

"That doesn't mean he's a mistake. Maybe I don't want—"

His fingers drifted over her butt, feather-light and almost nonexistent. "Was he me?"

"N-No." She bit down on her lower lip. "But—"

He pressed her against the wall, his leg slipping in between hers. "Then he was a big fucking mistake."

Chapter Ten

Holt rolled his knee against her core, grinning when she moaned and clutched at his shoulders. Her sharp nails dug into his skin, and he loved every fucking second of it. Seeing her with that asshole on the dance floor, grinning and smiling and having fun, had sent him over the edge.

Especially since the punk obviously thought he was going to be going home with her. He wasn't. Little fucker.

Seeing her flirting and dancing had only driven home the point he'd had in his head earlier: If she was going to be with a dickhead, why couldn't it be *him*?

He could be her dickhead.

At least he'd try to do his best not to hurt her.

"I missed you, Lyd." It had been only a couple of days since he'd walked away from her, but it had felt like a fucking lifetime. "Did you miss me?"

She made one of those sexy little sounds in the back of her throat. "What are you doing? I thought you wanted to be friends?"

"Friends do this," he muttered, nipping on her ear.

"Not mine." She stiffened and shoved at his shoulders. "What's going on, Holt?"

"I can't stand it. Seeing you with another guy, any other guy, isn't acceptable. I can't do it, can't just be your friend. I take it back."

Her fingers tightened on him. Not pushing, but not pulling him closer, either. "You can't just —"

"Yeah, I can." He leaned into her, trapping her against the wall. "And I am."

She bit down on her lip. "So what are you saying?"

"I'm saying I want to bring you home and fuck you until you stop thinking about other guys. I want to claim you. Own you. Make you come more times than ever before." He bit down on her shoulder at the same time he cupped her breasts, squeezing them. "And I won't leave before finishing this time."

"Just for tonight?" she asked.

"I don't know," he admitted honestly. "All I know is we're not finished yet. I can feel it all the way to my bones. Can't you?"

She nodded. "I can."

"Good." He ran his thumbs over her nipples. They were hard and aching for his touch. "Then let's keep doing what we're doing until we don't have that feeling anymore. Until we're finished."

"What about Steven?" she asked breathlessly.

Holt hesitated, still not entirely okay with that part of their situation. "He doesn't need to know. Do you need him to know?"

She shook her head. He didn't see it, but he felt it. "God, no."

His chest tightened. He didn't want to tell Steven, but she *really* didn't want to. And it made him wonder why. "Good."

"But are you sure? I don't want you to start, and then leave before we…you know. Finish."

He dropped his head into her neck. He'd sooner cut off his left leg than leave her naked and wanting in bed again. "I'm not leaving like that again, Lyd."

"Are you sure?" She nudged him. "Because if you get me all hot and bothered again, then take off…I'll legit kill you."

He snort-laughed. "I'm sure. But make no mistake: I'm done fighting this attraction between us because I'm not good enough to try anymore. Done trying to be the good guy by keeping my hands off of you. But that doesn't make me better. It makes me worse. You should say no. You should turn me away."

She stood there silently, and he held his breath. Half of him wanted her to say no, and the other half of him wanted her to say yes. One half was louder than the other. "I already told you earlier. If you'll knock, I'll let you in."

He dropped his forehead on hers. "Well, I'm knocking."

"Then come in. I'm waiting for you."

He kissed her, right there in the hallway in a crowded bar. He shouldn't start anything right now. He should hold her hand and bring her back to his place, while whispering sweet words to her. He should woo her. But instead, he wanted to make her come, with his name on her lips like some sort of fervent plea. He *needed* to.

Fuck the Tootsie Pop.

I want to know how many licks it takes to get to the center of Lydia.

The skirt she wore was ridiculously short—part of what had driven him crazy while she'd been on the dance floor—so he dropped to his knees in front of her and dragged it up. She gasped, her hands falling on his head. "What are you doing?"

"No one comes back here because it's a staff hallway, and I locked it. I owe you for last night, when I left, and it's time for me to pay." With one finger, he pulled her panties to the side. They were soft and lacy. It made him wonder what color they were, because it was too dark for him to see. "Hold on tight, Lyd."

She dug her hands into his hair, holding on tight as ordered.

Gently, he raised her leg and rested it over his shoulder. He could already smell her sweet scent. Feel her intoxicating heat. Leaning in, he flicked his tongue over her clit. She was better than anything he'd ever tasted before. Even more so than the water he'd chugged after being stuck in the one hundred and ten degree hell that they called a desert for eight hours.

She moaned, the noise mixing in with the loud music from the club. Her nails dug into his scalp, and she pressed against him, her hips moving restlessly. "Oh my God, Holt."

He deepened the intimate kiss, moving his tongue in circles over her. He could feel her whole body getting tighter, more frantic, and he knew she was close.

Hell, he could taste it, too.

Her hips moved faster, so he thrust a finger inside of her, crooking it just right. She arched her back, one of those sexy as fuck moans coming out, and then she froze, her heel pressing into his back. Afterwards, she collapsed against the wall, her body going lax.

Standing up, he swiped his hand across his mouth, pulled her skirt back into place, and caught her hand. "Come home with me tonight?"

"As if you needed to ask?" she said, laughing lightly. "Yes. God, yes."

He nodded once, even though she couldn't see him, and led her back into the crazy madness of the bar. As they worked their way across the floor, he caught sight of Paul, the dick she'd been dancing with earlier. He watched her leave, looking like a deflated puppy, but she didn't even glance Paul's way.

She was too busy watching *him*.

Thank fucking God.

As they walked into the night, she followed him silently. He'd die to hear her thoughts, to know what she was feeling right now. "You okay?"

"Mm hm." She smiled up at him. "I'm more than okay, because you just did amazing things with your mouth."

A smartass reply came to mind, but he couldn't get it out.

The words all jumbled in his head. He curled his hand into a fist. She'd said he'd done amazing things with his mouth. At least he could still get some things right. Since his mind had bailed on him, he remained silent.

A building pressure sprouted behind his forehead, making him wince. Shit, he was getting the headache a few days earlier than usual. And he'd already invited her home with him. If he tried to back out now, she'd think he was running.

He wasn't.

Maybe if he took the pills soon enough, he'd be okay. Maybe he'd be able to tuck her in to bed, and then suffer in silence while she slept.

"I'm glad you came to your senses," Lydia said, still smiling. "Giving up something that good is sacrilegious."

Guilt slammed into his chest. She thought it was a good thing he'd given in to his primal urges to claim her as his. She was wrong. She'd be much better off if he didn't. Hell, he could barely form a coherent thought on the best of days. And she was about to see his fucking worst. He opened his truck door for her. "A-After you."

"Okay." She hesitated, resting a hand over his heart. It was as if she already knew how strong of a hold she had over him, and was taunting him by placing her hand over the one part of him that she hadn't laid claim to yet. "But before I go with you, I need a promise."

Fuck me. He gritted his teeth, his head aching even more than just moments before. He didn't make promises to anyone. Not after the last one had led to him killing a good friend on a battlefield deep in the bowels of hell. "Tell me what you want."

"When you decide that feeling that we aren't finished yet is gone, just come to me. Be honest. Don't run. Don't hide behind your alleged shortcomings, and act as if you're doing me a favor by running. If you want to be done, we'll be done. But don't run without saying a word."

"I won't." He cradled her cheek. "When we're done, I'll let you know. I can't promise you forever. I can't promise you a long time. Hell, I can't even promise you tomorrow. But I can promise not to leave you without a proper goodbye."

She nodded. "That's all I ask."

"Then get in the truck, so I can take you home."

She climbed in, and he gave her a boost on the ass. She grinned over her shoulder at him, and he forced himself to smile back as if he didn't feel like he was about to die. The way she made him feel…it was like listening to a mash-up of warning bells and happy elevator music on repeat, which was confusing as hell.

He didn't know whether to push her away, or pull her close.

So he did both.

With a *hopefully* carefree wink, he shut the door. The bang made him flinch. A cold sweat already covered his forehead. This was going to be a bad one. He'd have to pop a pill as soon as they walked in the door, and grit his teeth through the pain. He slipped into his seat and kicked the truck into gear, his palms sweaty.

When he glanced over at her, she looked absolutely gorgeous in the moonlight. The streetlights bounced off of her, playing with the shadows, and it only highlighted her generous lips and high cheekbones even more than before.

An urgency that had nothing to do with his headache hit him like a punch in the gut. He'd already had her once, which should have been enough to temper the need rushing through him, but if anything, it only made it worse.

He had to have her, and he had to have her *now*.

Earlier, he'd told her they had to keep at it until the feeling was gone…but what if it never went away? He shuddered and tightened his grip on the wheel.

That was the closest he'd ever come to thinking in terms of long-term, and it was sickening as hell. But what made him even sicker was this next thought:

What if she tired of *him* before he tired of *her*?

Shit, that wouldn't happen, would it? He stole a quick glance at her, the movement sending a shaft of pain piercing through his skull. She stared out the passenger window, tapping her nails on her thigh. There had to be a way to make sure that didn't happen. A way to make her so addicted to him that she'd never think of leaving, but not so hooked that he broke her heart when he left.

Orgasms. Lots of them.

That had to work.

"When we get back to my place, you'll have one minute to be naked in my bed, waiting for me. If you're not there in time…" He drifted off, letting her imagination go wild with that one. *And while you scramble into my bed, I'll grab a pill out of the kitchen and hope to hell it works fast for once.*

She licked her lips and lifted her skirt a fraction of an inch. "Yes, sir."

"Good girl."

He rested his hand on her thigh possessively. She was so smooth. So small. So his. She pressed her thighs together, squeezing his hand in between them. "Sometimes."

His lips twitched. "Occasionally."

"Every once in a blue moon."

"Never," he added.

She inched closer. "Like right now."

"What are you going to do right now?" he asked, side-eyeing her.

"You'll see." She rested her hand on his cock. "Know my favorite moment between Rose and the Doctor? It's when they get trapped on opposite sides of the wall, in two different worlds." As soon as she finished talking, she squeezed him.

His headache was instantly forgotten. "Jesus, Lydia."

"That moment of complete and utter loss?" Slowly, she undid the zipper, brushing her fingers across him as she did so. "Yeah. That's the best few minutes of the show. And when he burns up the sun to say goodbye, but doesn't get to say he loves her?"

He swallowed hard, keeping his attention on the road by force of sheer will and nothing else. His vision blurred, so he blinked a few times to clear it. "Yeah?"

She freed his cock from his pants, and ran her fingers over it. "Heartbreaking. I mean, I bet they never even had the chance to do something like this…"

"*Lydia*."

She lowered her mouth to his cock, flicking her tongue over the head. He was hard and aching for her. Had been since the second he'd seen her in the club. Wait, no. He had been since he'd walked away from her, leaving her naked and alone on her bed.

With a groan, she closed her mouth over him and sucked him in. Her hot little mouth was pure heaven and hell, all wrapped up in one. He threaded his hand through her soft hair. They were almost at his place. *Almost.*

When she took more of him in, more than anyone else ever had before, he groaned and tightened his grip on her hair. "Shit, don't stop."

She didn't. She sucked harder, taking the rest of him in her mouth. He almost died, right then and there, from sheer pleasure. That's how fucking amazing it felt.

He turned into his driveway on two wheels, screeching tires and not giving a damn. Once he slammed the truck into park, he arched his hips up, fucking her mouth. He didn't hold back, not because he didn't care, but because he was too fucking gone to think. To worry.

Moaning, she sucked harder, scraping her teeth over the head and running her fingers over his balls, taking all he gave and then some more. He banged his head back against the headrest, sending even more pain coursing through him, and let out a string of curses he didn't even hear or mean to say.

For all he knew, he released a jumble of words that made no sense at all. It wouldn't be the first time. There was a reason he held himself back in bed.

Once, when he'd first returned from the war, he'd lost control. After he'd come, he'd collapsed on the bed next to the faceless woman he'd been with that night. She'd looked at him as if he was a monster. Apparently, his words had gotten mixed up in the heat of the moment, and it had freaked her out. She'd been out of his life within two minutes. He'd never lost control again.

Not until now.

He collapsed against the seat, her mouth moving over him until he was sure he'd go insane from the pleasure. Her sweet tongue brushed against him, and the way she moved her fingers, touching in all the right places, would surely be his cause of death. He couldn't think of a better fucking way to go. He arched his hips again, tugging on her hair. "I'm gonna come."

She nodded and kept going. He hadn't expected her to want to swallow…but he sure as hell wasn't going to complain. He watched her mouth move over him, clenched his jaw, and came explosively.

Words flew out of his mouth, and he dropped his head

back against the seat. She pulled off of him slowly, her mouth leaving a trail of torture behind. He hissed and tightened his grip on her hair, pulling her up. "*Enough.*"

Glancing away, he took a deep breath. He didn't want to see the look on her face, in case he'd lost his shit. From the corner of his eye, he watched her as she sat up, holding her hand over her mouth. He could feel her bright hazel eyes on him. She stayed silent, which was pretty damn damning, in his opinion. He'd fucked up. Again.

This was why he was better off alone, damn it.

"Lydia…" He took a deep breath and formed his thoughts as best as he could with his head throbbing like a bitch. And then he looked at her. She hadn't moved. "Look, I'm sorry if I scared you. If you want me to take you home…"

She blinked. "Scared me? Why would you have scared me?"

"Well, I…uh…"

She rested her hand on his arm. "There's nothing you've done, or could do, that would send me running. I was simply quiet because I was thinking how that was one of the hottest moments of my life, and I never want to forget a second of it."

"You're too good for—" He took a shaky breath and rubbed his temples. There was so much he wanted to say to that, but he couldn't even finish a damn sentence. His mind had quit on him, and now he was going to make a fool out of himself. "Shit."

"Are you okay?"

He nodded, turning away from her. He didn't need to see her pity, or fear, or anything, really. He just wanted to crawl under the covers and hide from the whole world.

Just wanted to disappear, until he felt human again. "I have to...I..."

"Lie down?" she asked softly.

"Yes. That."

Her door closed behind her, and for a second he thought she left him. He wouldn't blame her if she did. But then his opened, and her hands were on him. "Come on. I'll help you inside."

Disgust at what he'd become hit him hard. This wasn't him. He wasn't the guy who needed help, damn it. And her doing this was both amazing and frustrating, all in one. He didn't want to be this guy with her. He wanted to be the guy who blew her mind with amazing orgasms. The guy she missed when he was gone. The guy she needed...

Not the guy who needed *her*.

Chapter Eleven

Lydia watched him, forcing herself to stand completely still. He sat in the driver's seat, an array of emotions crossing his features. She knew, deep down, that he hated feeling the way he was right now. That he was two seconds from snapping, and she didn't want to be the one that pushed him too far. But he obviously needed help.

She didn't know what was wrong with him, or why he'd shut her out like that after she'd gone down on him, but she knew one thing: He was in pain, and he needed help. *And I need to give it to him.*

"*Go.*" He slammed his hand down on the wheel, and she jumped. "Go…home."

"No."

"Listen, little girl. You—" Gripping the wheel, he flexed his jaw, paling. After a few seconds, he swung on her, his blue eyes narrow and icy cold. "Get the hell out of here. I don't want you—"

She growled under her breath. "Stop right there," she snapped, lifting her chin.

"No. I don't want you here." He gripped the wheel even tighter. "Don't want you... I'm done. Get the...message."

Shaking her head, she crossed her arms. "You can't scare me away by being a jerk. I grew up with Steven—you're nothing compared to him. Get out of the truck so I can get you inside. *Now*."

He stared at her, breathing heavily. "I don't want you. Don't you hear me? Get the hell out of here."

"Nope." She put her hands on her hips. "I understand you're frustrated, and feeling like crap. But hear me and hear me well. I will not leave you until you're better."

"I'm never going to be—" He broke off, gritting his teeth. He was starting to look less pale, and more green. "— Better."

"Then you'll never be better. But I'm still not leaving."

"You little—" He gripped the steering wheel tighter, and the fight seemed to leave him. He collapsed against the seat. "—S...shit."

She swallowed hard. It hurt to see him hurting, and it hurt even more that he didn't want her there. "I just want to help you. Can't you see that?"

He nodded once, not replying. After what seemed like an eternity of silence, he let go of the wheel. "I need to get inside," he rasped.

"Okay." She caught his hand. "Let's go."

After a moment's hesitation, he entwined his fingers with hers and turned back to her. Pain and regret and something else she couldn't name were written all over his face, and almost made her fall over. He swallowed hard. "Lydia..."

"Shh. Come on."

He climbed out of the truck silently, his fingers still entangled with hers. Reaching into the truck, she grabbed his keys out of the ignition and walked up to his door with him. His silence was both a relief and a worry. Would he go off on her again? Say rude things to try and scare her away? She didn't know, but it didn't matter.

She wouldn't leave until he was okay.

With trembling hands, she unlocked the door. As soon as she shut it behind her, she turned to him. "What do you need?"

"Pills." He collapsed against the door, his face pale. "Kitchen."

She hurried into the kitchen, her heart pounding. Next to the sink, beside an empty bottle of whiskey, was an orange container filled with prescription medication for migraine headaches, according to the label. So...he got migraines. That's what this was. After she got the meds in him, she needed to get him in a dark, quiet room, and get a cold compress on his head.

At least she knew what to do now.

Twisting the lid, she shook a capsule out onto her hand. After opening a few cabinets, she found the one that held glasses. By the time she came back into the foyer, he'd shrugged off his coat and kicked off his shoes. When he heard her coming, he dropped his head against the door again.

"Here." She held out the water, and he took it with a trembling hand. Next, she gave him the pill. "After you take these, we'll get you in bed."

He nodded once, tossed the pill in his mouth, and downed all the water.

As soon as he finished, she grabbed the glass out of his hand, set it down, and clutched his hand. "Can you make it up the stairs?"

He grit his teeth so hard she could hear them scraping against each other. "*Yes*. I'm not—a—" He didn't finish that thought. "*Fuck*."

Pressing her mouth into a thin line, she fell silent, knowing she was only annoying him. Plus, if he had a headache, then talking—hers and his—would hurt. Slowly, they made their way up the stairs. As soon as they entered his room, he let go of her and stumbled toward his bed. She watched him go, her heart in her throat with every step he took.

When he stumbled, she lurched forward, ready to catch him. "Oh my—"

He caught himself and threw a scowl over his shoulder at her. "I'm not a child."

"I know. I never said you were."

When he reached the bed, he sat down and then fell back, flinging an arm over his face. He swallowed hard, his Adam's apple bobbing. He didn't say anything.

Neither did she.

After what had to have been like twenty minutes of silence and awkward fidgeting in the corner on her part, she walked over to him. By now, the meds should have hit. "Is there anything else I can do? Would you like a cold compress?"

His hand balled into a fist. After a few moments, he said, "Unless you can make the last fifteen minutes go away…no. There's nothing else."

Okay, then. The meds had definitely kicked in. Before they had, he'd been unable to form a whole word, let alone an entire sentence. And when he'd come, he'd blurted out a bunch of words in the wrong order. She hadn't thought anything of it, but now…

What exactly had happened to him overseas?

"There's nothing to be ashamed of, Holt." Sitting down on the side of the bed, she brushed his hair off of his forehead. He flinched, but otherwise didn't react to her touch. "Lots of people get migraines."

"You can go home now." He still didn't move. "I'll pay for your cab. If you could reach in my coat pocket and get my wallet out, there should be cash."

Her heart twisted. "Holt…"

"Lydia."

Reaching out, she squeezed his hand. "Look at me."

He finally opened his eyes. The blue was cold and hard. He wanted her to leave, and she would. But he had to know that she didn't care that he got headaches, or couldn't form his words perfectly one hundred percent of the time. None of that mattered to her.

All that she cared about was him, and if he was okay.

"I know right now, you don't like me very much. I know you wanted to suffer alone, where no one could see you. I get it. And I know you want me to leave, so I will, even though I'd rather stay with you, in case you need anything else tonight. But nothing that happened here tonight has changed a thing." She squeezed his hand. "*Nothing*."

He rolled his wrist and flipped his hand palm up, closing his fingers around hers. "I'm…I'm sorry. I shouldn't have been mean. It was…" He paused and licked his lips. "Uncalled for."

She smiled. "It's okay. I'm a bitch when I get PMS, so I'll

make it up to you in a week or two."

A little laugh escaped him, but he cut it off quickly. "Ow."

"Sorry." She rested a hand on his cheek. "I'll go now."

When he didn't say anything else, she walked for the door. She was halfway through it when he said, "Lydia?"

She froze, a hand on the doorjamb. "Yeah?"

"No one else knows I get these. No one…" He cleared his throat. "Thank you."

Blinking back tears, she didn't face him. "You're welcome. And don't worry. Your secret is safe with me."

She walked out of the room, down the stairs, and into the night. She didn't take money from him, because she didn't need to. Her brother lived two streets over, so she'd just walk there. Truth was, she kind of needed the time alone to clear her head. Holt obviously had a heck of a lot going on, and no one else knew about it.

Where was his support person? His parents? Siblings? *Anyone*?

Even more importantly, where the hell was Steven, his best bud?

By the time she made it to his door, she was furious. She marched up the stone walkway, lifted her fist, and pounded on the door. When he didn't answer, she did it again. A few minutes later, she heard a scuffling sound, and then a muffled curse.

The door swung open, and Steven stood there wearing nothing but a pair of boxers, his ink, and a scowl. He had a Glock in his hand, and his hair stuck up in different places. Once he saw who stood there, he dropped his hand to his side and closed the door enough that he could step behind it. "Jesus, Lyd. What's wrong?"

"Nothing's wrong. But you know what? You're a—" She broke off, realizing at the last second that she couldn't yell at him. She'd promised not to tell anyone about Holt's pain, and she wouldn't. "I mean, I was at a friend's house, and I had to leave. Can I sleep here?"

He nodded. "Yes, of course. But are you okay?"

"Y-Yeah."

"Do I need to kick someone's ass?"

She shook her head and slipped her coat off. She'd never even taken it off at Holt's. Everything had happened so fast. "No, I'm fine. I just need to sleep."

"Okay…" He set the gun down and wrapped her in his arms. "Lyd, are you sure you're okay? Where were you?"

"At a friend's house," she said, resting her cheek on his chest. "But don't ask who. It doesn't matter."

He tensed. "Actually—"

"*Steven.*"

He sighed. "Fine. But I'll be asking more questions to-morrow morning."

"Ask what you want, but I'm not talking." She stepped back. "The usual room?"

"Yeah." He ran his hands through his hair. "You might not want to look in my room as you pass. I left the door open…and, uh…"

She froze halfway up the stairs, because that meant he had a girl in his room, just days after splitting with his girl-friend of a year. "Seriously? Already? Who is she this time?"

He crossed his arms. "Whose house were you at tonight?"

"Touché." She headed up the stairs without answering… which was exactly what he'd intended, of course. "Good night."

"Oh, and sis?"

She stopped at the top of the stairs and glanced at him. "Yeah?"

"Next time, you might want to make sure your skirt isn't tucked into your underwear before leaving a guy's house in a hurry."

Her heart skipped a beat and she hurried to fix it. "Oh my God. No—" But when she touched her skirt, it was smooth and *not* stuck in her underwear. He scowled up at her, and she scowled right back at him. "*Steven.*"

"Just as I thought. Not a friend's house after all."

"It's none of your business what I do with my free time," she hissed, her cheeks hot. She'd fallen for the oldest trick in the book.

"Yeah, we're *definitely* going to be talking about this guy tomorrow." He raised a brow. "But hey, sleep well."

Without another word, she trudged into the guest room and shut the door. As soon as she was alone, she pressed a hand to her chest, reliving every moment…both good and bad…from tonight. About Holt. He'd been so playful at first.

So free.

And then, *bam*, the headache from hell had attacked him, and he'd been a different man. And everything from that point on had been awful. He'd even said some awful things, in his pain—not that she held that against him. She might not know much about Holt and his circumstances, but she knew one thing. He was alone, and he needed help. More than likely, the migraines and difficulty to form words came from the brain injury that Steven had told her about, and he was miserable because of it. She had a feeling he'd been accustomed to being perfect, and being anything less just made him hate himself. But he didn't need to be perfect to be loved.

No one did.

If she wasn't careful, *she'd* be the one to love him, and he would push her away. He might only be looking for a "for now" arrangement between them, but her feelings for him were growing too deep, too strong, too soon. If she wasn't careful…

He just might break her heart.

But that wouldn't stop her from giving herself to him anyway.

Chapter Twelve

Holt ran his hands through his hair and stared down at his phone. He wanted to call Lydia, but last night he might have blown any chances he'd had of being with her. Not only had he been weak, but he'd been an asshole, too. Two things women generally didn't find attractive. So…yeah.

But that didn't stop him from longing to call her anyway.

His head still had that dull ache he was all too fucking familiar with, but he felt mostly human. And a lot of that had to do with Lydia's care. She'd given him his meds, put him in bed, and made sure he was all right. She would have stayed longer, too, but he'd made her leave. Hadn't wanted her to see what came next—the vomiting.

He ran his thumb over the screen. "Son of a bitch."

Shoving his phone into his pocket without breaking down and calling her, he opened his truck door and walked up the path to Steven's house. He'd asked Holt to stop by this morning, so he walked in without knocking, like he always did. But as soon as he stepped foot inside, he froze. Steven wasn't alone.

"But you have to—"

"No, I don't," Lydia said, her voice hard. "I don't have to tell you a single thing, if I don't want to. And I don't want to."

"Just tell me his name. That's all I want."

She scoffed. "Who he is doesn't matter. We're just…you know, having fun. It's nothing important, or I would tell you who he was. He's nothing."

Holt tightened his fists. Yeah, they'd decided not to tell anyone else about their secret affair, but it still stung to hear it coming from her lips. He was two seconds away from barging in there and demanding she tell Steven the truth…which was crazy as hell.

Just like me.

"So, he's, what exactly?" Steven asked. "A booty call?"

"Call it what you want. It's just a temporary arrangement between the two of us. That's all."

Steven sighed. "And then once it's over, you'll go back to dating guys you can actually bring home?"

It sounded like she stomped her foot. "Steven, I don't like—"

Not wanting to hear the rest of that statement, Holt cleared his throat and stepped into the room. "Am I interrupting something?"

Lydia's cheeks suffused with color. She still wore the same outfit she'd had on last night, and her hair was a bit frizzy. Also, her face was devoid of makeup. He'd never seen her looking so fresh before. Gorgeous.

And so off-limits.

Steven turned to him, his cheeks red, too, but with anger,

not embarrassment. "No, we were just having a little talk."

"About?" he asked, cocking a brow.

"Inappropriate boyfriends."

Lydia turned even redder. "I never said he was my boyfriend. He isn't."

"Who has a boyfriend?" he asked, playing along. But the game made him feel sick to his stomach. "I didn't know you were seeing anyone special, Steven."

"Fuck you," Steven shot back. "I told you, if I was going to date a dude, I'd date you. But as it is, I still prefer chicks."

Holt snapped his fingers. "Damn."

"Wait." Lydia rubbed her head. "What?"

Steven snorted. "Don't even think about it. He might be my type, but he's not yours. He's too damn stubborn and dirty for a little girl like you." He slapped Holt on the back, sending a shard of pain through his skull. "Right, man?"

Of course he was right. But again, Holt wasn't that much worse than any other dude out there. He just…got migraines and couldn't always form his words properly. That wasn't so bad, was it? He winced. *Yeah, it was.*

"Right," Holt said between his clenched teeth.

"Are you okay?" Lydia asked, coming forward.

"Yes." Holt locked gazes with her. "I'm fine."

"Why wouldn't you be?" Steven looked at them both, no longer looking quite as jovial as before. "What did I miss here? What's going on?"

"Nothing. Just a headache," Holt said quickly. "I mean, just, uh…I—"

Lydia stepped forward. "When he drove me home the other night, he told me he gets headaches every once in a while. Said he felt one coming on, so I was asking about it.

That's all."

Holt blinked at her. She'd been quick to jump in and make sure Steven didn't see anything between the two of them. But in doing so, she'd given away information he didn't like giving out. Damn it. If people at work knew he was having headaches, and episodes, he'd never be able to keep his job. He'd already lost one position due to his injury.

He wasn't about to lose another.

Steven eyed Holt. "You still get those? I thought they stopped."

"Uh…" He looked at Lydia, giving himself a second to form his thoughts. "I don't get them anymore. They stopped. I thought I was going to have another one, but then it went away. False alarm."

"Oh. Good."

Lydia crossed her arms. "Yeah."

He stared right the fuck back at her. If he didn't want to tell anyone he was having migraines and panic attacks and every other awful thing he had…then it was his own fucking business. She'd sworn to keep his secret, and she would.

Steven cleared his throat. "Anyway, I have to go to another morning meeting with my new supervisor, and I'm late. Can you maybe give Lydia a ride back to her place, Holt? It's why I called you over here."

"Yes, of course," he said.

At the same time, Lydia said, "I can call a cab."

"No."

"No," Holt said at the same time as Steven. It earned him a weird look from his best friend. "I mean, I don't mind."

Lydia nodded once. "All right."

Steven grabbed his bag and hugged Lydia. "Let me know

if you hear back from Ian. He's supposed to be calling you again today."

"Yeah." Lydia glanced at Steven, then back at Holt. "Of course."

Holt stiffened. Who the fuck was Ian? And why hadn't she mentioned him before? He nodded at Steven as he walked by, waiting to hear the door shut behind him. As soon as it did, he cocked a brow. "Ian?"

She nodded, smoothing her hair with a trembling hand. "Yeah."

"Is there something I need to know about this Ian guy?"

Lydia blinked. "No. He's nobody. Just some guy that… that Steven wants me to meet, is all."

"Is that so?"

She crossed her arms. "Yeah."

"Bullshit. He—" He shook his head at himself. What the hell did he think he was doing, demanding answers out of her? They weren't exclusive. They weren't *anything*, really. "Never mind. Forget I asked. Ready to go?"

"Yeah. Come on."

When they got to his truck, he helped her into it again, but his mind was elsewhere on the ride to her place. On this Ian guy, whoever the fuck he was. Was she seeing him, too? He'd beat the shit outta the guy, and then strangle him until he never even thought about approaching his Lydia again. *Shit*. He didn't even know the guy, but he was already fantasizing about kicking his ass. With a muttered curse, he pulled into her parking lot, his grip on the wheel even tighter than before.

She glanced at him, then sighed and opened her door. "Well, thanks for the ride."

"I'll walk you up."

She hopped down. "You don't have—"

"I said, I'll walk you up." He opened his door and shut it behind him. "And I will."

"All right." She shrugged. "Whatever floats your boat."

She floated his fucking boat, but she already knew that. "Your roommate come home yet?"

"No. She's coming back in a couple of days." She unlocked her door and stepped inside. He followed her in, closing the door behind him. He locked it, too. "Thanks for the ride," she said again.

He nodded and rocked back on his heels, taking in her apartment. The flowers he'd given her were in a vase on a table in the dining room. That day felt like lifetimes ago. "Why did you go to Steven's instead of going home?"

"I don't know."

"Did you tell him about what happened? About...my issue?"

"No. Of course I didn't." She crossed her arms. "First of all, I didn't mean to slip up earlier. I just saw you flinch, and before I thought it through, I was asking if you were okay."

He swallowed hard. "It's fine."

"And second of all, how could I have told him? He would have wanted to know why I was there, and what we were doing." She lifted a shoulder. "But really, I just wanted to walk somewhere to clear my head, so I did. And then I was all ready to yell at Steven for not taking care of you. But then I realized—"

"Hold on." He held a hand up and took a step closer to her. "You walked there alone, while I was in bed sick?"

She crossed her arms. "Yeah. I've been walking by

myself for a while now. About twenty-three years, actually."

"You know what I mean." He took another step toward her. Two more steps and she'd be in his arms, bent over. He hadn't been finished with her last night when that headache had struck him. And he wasn't finished now. "It was dark out."

Rolling her eyes, she dropped her arms to her sides. "You don't say? And here I thought it stayed light all day long, and I was just in a really big shadow."

"*Lydia*." Another step, and he grabbed her chin, tilting her face up to his. "You shouldn't do that kind of shit. What if something happened to you while I was unable to help?"

"I was fine." She grabbed his wrists, holding onto him but not pushing him away. "I can take care of myself."

"I know. But I want to." He paused, trying to form the words perfectly. "Take care of you. Like you did for me."

She licked her lips. "You do?"

"I do." He ran his thumb over her jawline. She was so soft and smooth. So very different from him. "I know a great way to do that, actually. Unless that Ian guy would object…"

"It's not like that," she said softly. "He's nothing to me, not like you. He's just some guy who wants me to—"

"Shh." He lowered his lips to hers, stopping just short of touching. He hauled her closer by pressing a hand to her lower back. She surged against him, every tantalizing inch of her body touching his. "It doesn't matter who he is, and I have no right to be a jealous prick over it. For now, you're mine, and I'm yours. That's all that matters."

He backed her against the red wall that led into her kitchen, right next to her bookshelf. It was true. The future and the past weren't important.

All that mattered was *this*.

"You're jealous?" she asked, dipping her fingers down his chest, over his belt buckle, and then cupping his hard cock. She could barely squeeze her hand in, because he was pressed up so tightly against her. "I thought you didn't get jealous?"

He kissed her, knowing it was enough of an answer. Besides, he didn't think he could give her a straight reply when her hand was on his dick. As he kissed her, she undid his pants with trembling hands and flicked her tongue over his.

It almost sent him over the edge, just that simple gesture. This undying need to have her, to make her his, in every sense of the word, wasn't getting any weaker. And that was scary. Despite his attraction to her, he didn't fool himself into thinking they had anything worth trying to keep. She needed a better man than him.

No, she *deserved* a better man than him.

But he could be good enough for now.

He swept her into his arms and carried her to her bedroom, his lips never leaving hers. Hell, if he stopped kissing her, he'd die. That's how much he needed her. It was both scary and new. As soon as they cleared the bedroom door, he tossed her onto the bed, following her down on it and ravishing her mouth even more.

She wrapped her arms around his neck and held on tight, making those hot little whimpering sounds he loved so fucking much. This time, he wouldn't lose control. This time, he would remain sane and not spew out a shitload of words that made no sense.

But when she slid her hand inside his pants and closed

her small hand around his cock…all thoughts fled. Growling, he deepened the kiss and shoved his hand up her skirt. The second he touched her wet heat, he was a goner. He could sit there and say he was going to remain in control until he was blue in the face, but the truth was, around her…

He couldn't.

"Shit," he muttered, thrusting a finger inside of her.

She cried out, arching her hips. He could make her come right here, right now, with a finger. But he wanted to be buried inside of her when she came.

He pushed off of her and stood, his hands on his pants. "No."

"What?" She blinked and sat up partially, pouting, and she looked two seconds from either hitting him or crying. Maybe both. "What do you mean, *no*?"

"Stand up," he said, letting his pants hit the floor. Slowly, he took off his glasses and set them on the nightstand. "Now."

She bit down on her plump lip. "Yes, sir." Rolling to the side, she stood in front of him within two seconds flat, her hand resting over his heart. "Now what?"

Lifting his hand, he spun his finger in a circle. "Turn around."

Her lips parted on a ragged breath, but she did as he asked immediately. Once she faced away from him, she peeked over her shoulder with sultry eyes. "Sir?"

"So eager." Reaching around her, he gripped the bottom of her silk shirt in a tight ball and tugged her back against his chest. Nibbling on her ear, he murmured, "So fucking sweet, too."

She arched her neck for him, granting him access. "*Holt*."

He yanked her shirt over her head, grinning at her

surprised gasp. Dropping it to the floor, he undid her bra and let that fall, too. Splaying his hand over her stomach, he rolled his hips against her ass, loving how soft she felt against his cock. "Yeah, Lyd?"

"P-Please." She gripped his thighs, pressing against him.

"Not yet." He tugged her skirt down over her generous hips, watching hungrily as more and more of her skin became visible. When the skirt hit the floor, she wore nothing but a thong and her long hair. He curled his fist into those soft locks, tugging her head back. "But don't worry. I'll be buried inside you soon. And you'll never want me to leave."

"I'm already worried about that," she whispered, pressing her thighs together.

His grip on her hair tightened. "What?"

"Never mind."

He tugged harder. "Answer me. *Now*."

"I said I'm already worried I'll never want you to leave," she said, her voice soft and heated. "Happy now?"

Satisfaction hit him. That, and…yeah, fucking *happiness*. He wasn't going to lie.

She liked him and didn't want him to leave yet, and that was a good thing, because he didn't want to leave yet, either. He smacked her ass gently, grinning when she cried out. "Actually, yes."

"Then what was that for?"

"Talking back to me. You know you're not allowed to do that." He rubbed the spot he'd struck, soothing away any lingering pain. "Don't act as if it's actually a punishment. We both know it's not."

He pulled her hair again until her head was tipped back, and bit her neck at the same time as he smacked her ass again. She whimpered. "Oh my—*Holt.*"

My Holt. He liked the sound of that. Slipping his finger under her thong, he slid it across her stomach and stopped just above her core. "Do you have protection here?"

"Yeah. Top drawer."

Without letting go of her, he opened the drawer and pulled out a condom. "I won't ask why you have these in your room, since you were practically a virgin before you were mine."

"I wasn't screwing guys, but that doesn't mean I was a nun." She glanced over her shoulder. "Believe it or not, I've been in this bed with a man before. Not—"

Growling, he gently shoved her face first on the bed. "Enough of that. I don't want to hear a single fucking word about the other men you've known."

"If you say so," she said, wiggling her ass. Her hand disappeared under her body, and she touched herself. He could see her fingers peeking through from between her legs. "I need you, Holt. *Hurry.*"

He smacked her again, and she grinned. Actually fucking grinned. Jesus, she was going to kill him. And he'd never find someone who turned him on as much as she did, either. No matter how long he searched, or how far. She moaned and her fingers moved over herself faster, making his stomach tighten and his dick get uncomfortably hard.

Slipping the condom on his cock, he gritted his teeth. "Lydia."

"Please," she whimpered, tilting her ass up even more. Her fingers never stopped moving. "*I need you.*"

Slowly, oh so fucking slowly, he lowered her thong. Gripping her hips, he positioned himself behind her. "Then hold on tight, because you have me."

Her hand curled into her comforter, and he thrust inside of her with one hard, fast drive. She was so tight and wet and hot. But when she writhed beneath him, a cry escaping her, he forgot all about that. "*Harder—please.*"

He froze, his grip on her hips softening. Hell, he'd just barged into her like a fucking newbie. He should have been easier on her. Gentler. "Are you...Did I...?"

"You didn't hurt me." She smacked the bed, her entire body practically throbbing with frustration. "Now keep going. And don't you dare stop again."

Oh, he wouldn't. As a matter of fact, he never wanted to stop...

And that was fucking terrifying. More so than being lost in enemy territory, with no one to come help him. He tipped her hips up and withdrew, gritting his teeth when her body tried to pull him back in. She moved her hand out from underneath of her, but he grabbed it. "No. Keep touching yourself. Don't stop."

She whimpered, but did as told. As soon as she had her fingers on her clit, he moved his hips, driving inside of her again. She was even tighter now, and she made those whimpers that meant she was close to coming already. Reaching around her, he added his fingers to hers, helping her get herself off.

His other hand covered hers, entwining their fingers on the bed. She stiffened beneath him, clinging to his hand tightly. "I'm going to—*yes.*"

The words died on her lips, and she came. Her walls squeezed him, and she tried to pull back. He pressed down on her, leaving their hands against her clit, and fucked her.

Nonsensical words escaped her, words that made no sense.

He'd never heard anything more beautiful.

Burying his face in her hair, he groaned and moved his hips faster, resting his weight on his elbows. "Fuck, Lydia. You're going to kill me, you know that?"

She nodded frantically. "I can't…no, don't stop. More, more, *yes*."

Her entire body went hard, and she came again, clamping down on his cock with heavenly pressure. Sweat rolled down his forehead, and he lost all control. What little he'd had left, anyway. The faster he moved, the more she cursed and cried and strained to get closer to him. By the time he came, she was right there with him again.

Spent, he collapsed to the mattress, rolling and taking her with him. They ended up lying diagonally across the bed, her hand on his chest and a leg thrown over both of his. He covered her hand with his and kissed her temple. It was quiet and still…

And he had something he needed to say.

Chapter Thirteen

Lydia sighed, feeling more at peace than ever before. Ever since her brother had dropped the bomb on her that, through his buddy, Ian, he might have found a position for her down at a hospital in Delaware, she'd been a mess of emotions, not sure what she should do, or say, when Ian called her later today, as promised. And when Holt had asked who Ian was, she'd frozen and refused to answer, refused to tell him he was her potential boss…all the way down in Delaware. If she told him she might be leaving, and he didn't give a damn, it would hurt.

And she wasn't kidding herself. He *wouldn't* give a damn.

He played with a strand of her hair, his body gradually tensing beneath hers. Eying the clock, she saw it was close to eight-thirty in the morning. How it could be so early in the day, when so much had happened already, was beyond her.

She sighed. "Do you have to—?"

"Look, I'm sor—" he started at the same time, cutting

himself off when he realized they spoke at the same time. "Sorry, go ahead."

She shook her head. "You go first. I insist."

"Okay." He took a deep breath. "I wanted to say I'm sorry for last night. I felt the headache coming, but I'd been hoping I could take a pill and be okay before you noticed." He paused. "I was obviously wrong."

She shook her head. "I don't care. There's nothing to apologize for. You had a headache. There's nothing wrong with that."

"But there is. It's not just the headaches, Lyd." He took a deep breath and held it in. "When I'm having an episode — that's what they're called — for the days leading up to it, I can't function. My brain doesn't work properly. If my boss found out I still have those migraines, and that I can't do my job…"

She lifted up on her elbow and bit her tongue. He was opening up to her, and that was great. But she was scared if she pushed too much or too hard, it might scare him away. "So you only have the problems leading up to the migraines?"

"Mostly. When my words start getting mixed up, I know one's coming. I've gotten good at hiding it, and at dealing with the pain, but last night was particularly bad." He dragged a hand through his hair, staring up at the ceiling with a wrinkled brow. "It's basically like a slow build. It starts with having problems figuring out simple things. Then the words get all jumbled up in my head, and then a few days later…it escalates till I'm incapacitated. After that, it slowly gets better until the next time."

"What happened to cause it? Or has it always been like

this?"

He dropped his hand above his head. The other was wrapped around her waist. The sun hit his face, making his five o'clock shadow look even darker than before. "It happened the same place I got those scars. Same time, too."

And that was obviously all he wanted to say on that matter. He was very much like Steven in that regard. He never wanted to talk about the things he'd seen and done over *there*, either. She couldn't blame them. "I'm sorry."

He glanced down at her. "Did Steven ever mention anything?"

"Kind of." She licked her lips. "He mentioned you'd been injured over there and were struggling to fit back in to society, but I didn't ask for all the details. I figured if you wanted to tell me, that was fine, but if not, that was fine, too. I'm not going anywhere anytime soon."

He smiled and cupped her cheek. "You know, for the first time ever, I want it to stay that way. I don't want to lose you."

Her heart stuttered and sped up, all at once. Which, medically speaking, wasn't possible. "Don't say that too loudly. I might think you actually mean it."

The smile slipped off his face, and his bright blue eyes were bluer than she'd ever seen them before. "What makes you think I don't?"

Not knowing what to say to that, and quite frankly a little bit speechless, she leaned down and kissed him gently. By the time she pulled back, his grip on her was no longer gentle. It was possessive and demanding.

"It's almost nine," she whispered against his lips.

He groaned. "I know. I have to go before Steven realizes

I took way too long to get to work, and figures out why."

"Ugh." She rolled off of him and stared up at the ceiling. "All right. Go, before I change my mind and chain you to my bed."

He leaned on his elbow and smiled down at her. This man, naked, in her bed, smiling at her, was freaking dangerous as heck. "You can chain me to your bed anytime you want, Lyd. How's tonight sound to you?"

"It sounds…" Her heart sped up, because he traced a path around her bare nipple. "Y-You're coming over?"

"Hell yeah." He kissed her gently, and hopped off the bed. She watched him walk over to his discarded clothes. His body was hard and toned. She could literally count the muscles that made up the perfect image that was Holt. "That is, unless you don't want me to. I guess I should ask?"

She laughed. "Oh, I want you to."

"Good. Because I would have come anyway, and changed your mind with a few orgasms." He dressed quickly, and went into her bathroom. By the time he came back out, he looked as put together as he had before she'd stripped him. He wore grey khakis, a plaid shirt, and Converse sneakers. After he slipped his glasses on, he stared down at her with so much heat she should have combusted right there on her cotton sheets. "Stop looking at me like that, or I'll forget I have to go to work today, and spend all afternoon making you come."

"Hm. Is that supposed to be a threat?" She gave him what she hoped was her most sultry look ever. "Because it sounds more like a promise."

Growling under his breath, he slipped his hand behind her head and lifted her up so he could kiss her. His mouth moved over hers with a hypnotic perfection that only he could ever manage. It was no wonder she was so hooked on the guy. He knew exactly what to do to get her all hot and bothered, and he was gorgeous, to boot.

He pulled back and groaned. "You taste so fucking sweet. I'll be by around eight. Be naked and ready for me, or pay the price."

"Yes, sir," she breathed, anticipation already making her wet. "I'll be ready for you...and only you."

He made a sound of approval, and gently lowered her back down to the pillow. After one last long, heated look, he turned and left her alone in her bed.

She missed him already.

· · ·

Two nights later, a knock sounded on her door at nine o'clock sharp. Exactly when Holt had told her he'd be coming over. They'd spent every night together either at her place or his, since the morning he'd taken her home from her brother's house. Lydia had spent the day applying to open positions and fielding a few phone calls from a few more. So far, she'd had no luck at all...besides the position in Delaware. She'd spoken to her brother's friend, Ian, and he wanted to hire her. She had until tomorrow afternoon to decide whether or not to accept his generous offer.

And she still had no idea if she wanted to take it or not, but she had a pretty good idea what her answer would be. She'd lived in Maine her whole life. Her family was here. Her friends. Holt...

Yeah. Him, too.

They might not be a forever thing, but she liked him a lot, and she didn't want to leave before they were finished. Didn't want to leave him yet.

Opening the door, she smiled at him. "Hey. Sorry, it was a busy day filled with papers and phone calls and—"

Cupping her cheeks, he kissed her midsentence. Her arms flailed for a second, as she was completely caught off guard, but then she rested them on his chest and returned the kiss. By the time he pulled back, she'd forgotten what she'd been saying.

"Hey," he whispered, his forehead pressed to hers.

"Hi," she whispered back, fisting his shirt. "That was quite the welcome."

He let go of her and backed into the hallway, a hesitant smile on his face. He looked almost…nervous. "I'm not done yet. I got you something."

"Oh?"

Her roommate and best friend, Gianna, came out of her bedroom. "Sorry, just passing through."

Lydia cleared her throat. "Gianna, this is Holt. Holt, meet Gianna."

"Nice to meet you," Gianna said.

"Likewise," Holt said, smiling. "Sorry to barge in like that."

"Please." Gianna waved a hand and grabbed her purse. "It's fine. I'm leaving, anyway, so you guys will have the place to yourselves."

Lydia smiled. "See you later."

"You too." She wiggled her fingers as she slipped out into the hallway. "Don't do anything I wouldn't do."

Once she was gone, Lydia stared at Holt, who cleared his

throat. "She seems nice."

"She is." Lydia tapped her fingers on her thigh and peeked out the door. "What were you saying earlier about not being done?"

"Oh. Right." He reached down for something on the floor in the hallway, but didn't pick it up. "You have been good to me when I've been cranky, surly, and at times... standoffish. So when I saw this, and it made me think of you, I just had to get it. As a thank you."

She blinked, holding a hand to her heart. "Okay. You didn't have to get me anything, though. I took care of you because..." *I care about you.* "...it was the right thing to do."

"And so was this. You deserve to be treated like a princess, Lyd." Swallowing hard, he pulled a big box out of the hallway. "This is only a tiny thing in comparison."

She reached out with trembling hands and took the box. It was wide and not all that heavy. She sat on the couch and ripped it open, more eager than a child on Christmas morning to discover what Holt had gotten her. She couldn't wait to see how—

"Oh my God." When she lifted the last piece of cardboard, she gasped out loud in delight. "It's Rose and Ten! On the wall! In parallel worlds!"

Holt relaxed, a grin taking over his previously intense expression as he'd watched her open the present. "Yep. I remembered you saying you liked that moment..."

Heart racing, she stared down at the drawing, blinking back tears. He'd gotten her a lovely depiction of her favorite couple from *Doctor Who*, in her favorite scene. The fact that he'd remembered her passing remark about this being her favorite part of the show made her heart melt. Heck, it made *her* melt.

She should literally be a puddle of goo at his feet right now.

"This is…" She trailed her fingers over the glass, staring down at David Tennant and Billie Piper. "Perfect. It's just perfect. Thank you."

He sat beside her and rested a hand on her thigh. "No, thank you. For way too long, I've believed that being alone was the thing for me. That I couldn't trust anyone, or let anyone in. But then I met you, and for the first time ever…I want to do it. I want to let you in."

She gripped the picture frame. "You mean…like, a real couple or something?"

"Yeah. Maybe. I don't know." He clasped her hand, entwining his fingers with hers. "I'm a hot fucking mess. I get migraines and nightmares, and I don't really believe in happy endings for guys like me. I've done horrible things I will never talk about."

"Holt…" she whispered, her heart wrenching. "You know—"

He held his hand up. "And, yes, I know you deserve more than I can give you, but will you be mine anyway?"

She blinked rapidly, fighting to keep the tears back, and set the picture down on the table safely. Turning to him, she framed his face with both of her hands. "Y-Yes. I'd love to be yours, but just so you know? I already was."

He dragged her onto his lap and kissed her, just as he'd done plenty of times before. But this time it felt different. As his mouth melded to hers, she melted into him, and figured out why it felt different. This kiss was filled with wonder and tenderness.

And so much more.

When he ended the kiss, he pulled back and smiled at her. "So it's official, then? We're dating?"

"I guess so," she said, running her thumb over his cheek-bone. "Now what do we do? Tell people?"

He groaned. "Can we not? I just know that this is all so new to me, and having your brother glaring over my shoulder as I try to figure out the way to be a good boyfriend..."

Part of her felt let down that he didn't want to tell any-one, like she was some dirty little secret or something, but the other part of her understood. Mostly.

"Then we won't tell anyone," she said, forcing a smile. "But at some point, provided you decide to stick around, we're going to have to let people know."

He looked more relieved at being let off the hook than she would have liked. "Okay, good. And we will tell them, eventually. I promise."

"Right." She swallowed hard and focused on the pic-ture again, trying to ignore the part of her that was upset. "Sounds good."

He captured her chin and turned it toward him. "Hey, why so sad?"

"I'm not sad," she said quickly.

"Yes, you are. Don't lie to me." His fingers flexed on her chin. "You want to tell Steven. That's what it is, right?"

She bit down on her lip. "Yeah. It's just...it almost feels like you're hiding me because you're ashamed. Like you don't want to admit you like his annoying little sister, or whatever."

"No. That's not it at all." He shook his head and sighed. "If anything, it's the other way around. I know you deserve better than me, and you can bet your ass Steven knows, too. Not to mention the fact that he specifically told me to stay the hell away from you. There's that, too."

She winced. "I know, and I get the bro-code. I do. But… if you really want to be with me…"

"I'd tell him," he finished flatly.

"Yeah. Pretty much."

He let go of her and dragged his hands down his face. "All right. I'll do it tomorrow at lunch. It's a Friday, so it'll give him the whole weekend to get over his urge to kill me before I see him again."

"Really?" she asked, her heart picking up speed. "Want me to be there?"

"No." He blew out a breath. "I think this is something that's better done on my own, in case he decides to kill me right away. You won't want to watch that."

She winced. "He won't kill you."

"Yeah, he probably will." A grin lit up his face, and he yanked on her legs till she was flat on her back on the couch. Without wasting a second, he was on her, his body covering hers. "But it'll be worth every single moment of pain. *You're* worth it."

And then he kissed her again.

Chapter Fourteen

An hour later, Lydia curled up with Holt in bed and yawned. After what they'd just done, she'd be limping for a few days, to say the least. But she'd be limping with a huge smile on her face. And maybe a sore butt cheek...

But again. Totally worth it.

She stared at her phone, nibbling on her lower lip. She'd finally come to a decision...mostly. She wasn't going to take the job in Delaware. Yes, it was a wonderful opportunity. One she was lucky to have. But she didn't want to live in Delaware.

Didn't want to leave her family.

Steven had been overseas fighting for the past five years, and she'd barely seen him during that time, had never known if he was alive or dead...or worse, captured. Now he was back, and he wasn't going anywhere. So why would she want to move away and miss out on being with him? He was the only family she had left. She didn't want to *leave* him, no matter how great the opportunity might be.

Plus, even though she and Holt were just starting out, she *did* like him. She wouldn't stay *for* him, but staying here would let her get to know him better.

Holt was simply the icing on the cake.

"You all right?" Holt asked, kissing the top of her head. "You're being quiet. That's an anomaly all by itself, but you're also sighing."

"I'm fine. Just…thinking."

He tugged on a piece of her hair. "About…?"

"Us. Life. Choices." She rested her chin on his chest and studied him, her concentration turning to his scars. "All sorts of things, really."

He followed her line of vision, a frown coming over his face. "Like my scars."

"Well, yeah." She blew her hair out of her face. "It's something I think about. I'm not going to lie. Not the scars, per se, but the things that caused them…and the ones I can't see."

He stiffened. "They're just marks from war. Nothing else."

"I know." She bit down on her lower lip. "But they *are* more. I can see the shadows that haunt you. I'm not blind, you know."

"Yeah, and they're going to stay where they belong—behind me. Buried and hidden and mine. Just mine." He shifted away from her, both mentally and physically. "They come with the nightmares, and the headaches, and the episodes."

She knelt beside him, refusing to back down. "I know. And it's all a part of you."

"Yeah, the bad parts," he muttered. "Stop looking at me

like that."

"Like what?"

"Like you want to fix me." He dragged a hand through his hair. "I can't be fixed with a tender conversation and a kiss. This is me. This is what you get. The good and the bad."

"I know that," she said, pressing her mouth into a tight line. "I wasn't implying I could fix you. As a matter of fact, I don't even think you need to be fixed at all."

He snorted. "Yeah, you do. That's a lie."

"I think you should tell people about your migraines, but that's about it."

He glowered at her. "So I can get fired for being unable to do my job properly? Yeah, that sounds like a great idea."

"You might not get fired, though." She curled her hands in her lap, forcing herself to remain still, because he kept pulling away from her when she pushed too hard. "Maybe, just *maybe*, your boss would understand, and give you time off when you needed it. If you rested when the episodes started up, instead of working through them, I bet they'd be more manageable. And you just might be more useful to him in the long run."

"I'm sure they would be very manageable," he said sarcastically. "Because I'd be out of a job half the month. Something tells me that Cooper, no matter how understanding he might be, wouldn't be okay with that. Just…just leave it, Lyd."

She held her hands up. "Fine. But you act like your condition is something to be ashamed of. Like your injuries are this awful thing you have to hide."

"Because they are." He stood up and grabbed his pants, stepping into them angrily. "You have no idea what I went through. What I did."

"You're right. I don't, because you've told me in no un-certain terms that you'll never talk to me about it. And that's fine. I would never force you to talk about something if you didn't want to." She crossed her arms, watching him dress. "But you can't throw it in my face how I don't understand if you don't want to talk about it."

He yanked his shirt over his head. "Obviously, you want to know all about it. Or we wouldn't be fighting about it."

Wait, what? "We're not fighting." She grabbed his hand. "We're not—"

He snorted. "I might not know much about relationships, but I know a fucking fight when I see one."

He's right. We're totally fighting. "Holt—"

"And I also know that fights always end with the man giving in, so fine. You…you want to hear all the gory details? Want to hear how I watched every single guy around me die? Want to hear how the one guy I was friends with, who I was closest with, begged me to finish him off as he bled out on the field?" Shoving his arms into his sleeves, he glared at her through his glasses. As he'd spoken, his voice got louder and louder until he was practically shouting at her. "The ani-mals were howling in the woods, so he knew it was only a matter of time till they came looking for food. And he didn't want to be alive for it."

Her stomach turned at the thought of what he'd gone through. What he'd seen…and yes, *done*. It wasn't too hard to guess whether or not he'd done what his friend had asked. "Holt…"

"I did it, you know. I put him out of his misery. I killed him." He locked gazes with her and sat down. "I did it because he asked me to, and I'd expect someone to do the same thing for me if I asked. But I have nightmares. Every. Fucking. Night. I relive it, *every night*. So why the hell would I want to tell you about it, so you can relive it, too? I wouldn't wish that on anyone. Especially not you."

She crawled across the bed and onto his lap. Straddling him, she hugged him. Just…hugged him. Because he seemed like he really needed a hug, and she wished she hadn't started this conversation in the first place. "I'm so sorry. So sorry you had to do that, and even sorrier that I kind of, sort of, forced you to tell me."

For a second, his arms hovered at his sides, as if he didn't know how to hug someone back. But then closed his arms around her and squeezed, letting out a broken breath. He buried his face in her neck and shook his head slightly. "I'm sorry I yelled at you. I…I didn't mean to."

"Shh." She rubbed his back, not daring to move. Not just then. He'd opened up to her, and then he'd stayed. That was huge, and she knew it. "It's okay."

He set his hands on her shoulders and tugged her back. "It's not…not really. You have a right to know, if we're going to make this thing between us real. You should know how much of a mess you're getting into."

Swallowing hard, she nodded. "Okay. Yeah. But I don't think you're a mess. And I never will. I think you've been through a lot, seen a lot, but that doesn't make you a mess. Or a bad guy. It makes you a hero."

He flexed his jaw. "Hell no. I'm not one of those."

"We'll have to agree to disagree." She forced a smile. "Because you'll never get me to change my mind."

"Now that you know what I did—*who* I am—do you…?"

He cleared his throat and swallowed. "Do you still want to try this? Because I'm not kidding when I say I have nightmares. I do."

Her heart twisted, but she forced her smile to remain firmly in place. "I drool. A lot."

"Uh?" he blinked. "That's not even close to the same thing."

Shaking her head, she somehow managed to look dead serious. "Sure it is. Wait till you roll over into a puddle of it in the middle of the night. Then say that it's not a deal breaker for you."

For a second, he stared at her. Then he laughed, and all of the worry and tension faded away. "Shit. What the hell am I getting myself into?"

"I don't know. You might want to run while you can."

"Uh uh." He tugged her until she laid flat on her back, and trailed his fingers down her bare skin. In all the emotions of the past few minutes, she'd forgotten that she was naked… while he no longer was. "I don't scare off that easily."

Her muscles clenched at his touch. "Are you sure?"

"Yes." He splayed his hand across her stomach. "It might be crazy to think that something like this could actually work, but you're stuck with me. I'm not going anywhere."

"Why would it be crazy?" she asked softly. He watched her, but wasn't really there. He seemed lost in thought. "What's so crazy about us being together?"

"You're shiny and clean. Wholesome and new." Gently, he trailed his thumb over her lower lip. "And I'm…not. Not even close. The two pieces don't fit together."

She shook her head. "That's where I think you're wrong."

"That doesn't make you right."

"One of us is," she argued, flicking her tongue out at his thumb. "It might as well be me."

His thumb pressed against her mouth. "Might as well be." Leaning down, he kissed her. By the time he pulled back, she was even more certain she was right. He lay down beside her again, staring up at the unmoving ceiling fan. "Lydia?"

She blinked sleepily. "Yeah?"

"Thank you." His fingers tightened on her. "Thank you... for making me talk. And for listening, without judging."

"I'd never judge you for something you've done. Or anything you do."

He flexed his jaw. "You have no idea what you're saying right now."

"Actually, I do. And I mean every word."

Sighing, he rolled to his feet and stood. "I have to go. You should get some rest."

"Can't you stay?" she asked, leaning up on an elbow. "You don't have to leave..."

"I-I have work to do," he said, rubbing the back of his neck. "But we'll talk tomorrow after...you know. Okay?"

She bit her lip and nodded. For some reason, it felt as if he was leaving her for good...instead of for tonight. "Okay."

"Don't look so sad." Leaning down, he pressed a fleeting kiss to her lips. "After tomorrow, the hard part will be over. Steven will know, and I'll be free to...well, shit. I don't know. Walk with you in the streets. Whatever people do when they announce they're a couple."

Her lips twitched. "The same thing you've done with other girlfriends."

"Nothing else scared you away, but this might. You see...I've never really had one before," he admitted, rubbing his jaw. "But I'll figure out what that all means after I tell Steven."

She blinked at him. "Wait. You've never had a girlfriend before? Like...*ever*?"

"Ever. I told you that you had no idea what you were getting yourself into," he muttered, avoiding looking at her. "Still want me to tell Steven?"

Swallowing hard, she nodded. "Of course. But can I ask one more question?"

"Yeah..."

"Why haven't you had a girlfriend?"

"As a kid, I was kind of nerdy." He rolled his eyes. "As if you didn't guess as much from my love for all things geeky."

She smiled. "Okay. And as an adult?"

"Well, I never met someone who made me want to settle down." He gazed at her. "Not until you."

Her heart skipped a few beats. "Oh."

"Yeah. Oh." He fisted his hands at his hips, staring her down, his whole body tense. He looked like he might snap if he tensed even a little bit more. "I like you, Lyd."

Smiling, she forced herself to remain calm and cool, when she wanted to jump on the bed like a kid and shout, "*He likes me!*" at the top of her lungs. "I like you, too, you know."

His muscles relaxed, and he laughed. "You don't say?"

"I totally do."

He grabbed his keys off the nightstand and shoved his phone into his pocket. "Then wish me luck with your brother. I'm going to need it tomorrow."

"Stop it." She fidgeted with the blanket. "He's not that bad..."

"Yeah." Holt snorted. "It's not as if he was a SEAL or anything."

She winced. "Okay. You *might* have a point."

"I know I do. But even if he kicks my ass…" He skimmed his fingers over her bare shoulders as he passed. "It'll be worth every bruise, sprain, or broken bone. See you tomorrow."

Lydia watched him go, her stomach a ball of nerves and excitement. Starting tomorrow, her life would really begin. While she might have fallen for him quickly, like she had in the past, this time there was no doubt in her mind that this was right. That they were meant to be. Sometimes, people fell quickly because they just *knew*. And she was one of them. She'd never been happier, really, so it made her decision a no brainer. She wasn't staying in Maine *because* of Holt…

But she wasn't going anywhere.

Chapter Fifteen

The next afternoon, Holt stepped into Steven's office and made himself smile. He'd promised to tell Steven about his feelings for Lydia at lunch, but he'd been too busy catching up on overdue work to eat. And if he was going to keep his promise to Lydia, then he needed to tell him. *Now*.

"It's about damn—" Steven glanced up, his eyes narrow. "Oh, it's you."

Holt raised a brow. "Who did you think I was?"

"My sister." He tossed a pen down. "She's late."

Fuck. Did she think he told Steven already? If so, he'd best get his ass in gear and open his mouth. "Oh. Right. I didn't know she was coming here." He cleared his throat and tugged on his collar. "There's something I have to tell you. I—"

Steven slammed his pen down on the desk. "This is just so unbelievable, and so fucking typical of her. Always flitting from relationship to relationship, falling in love as fast as she can say hello to a guy. Well, this is the last straw. She's in deep shit with me."

Wait. She fell in love all the time?

If that was true, and she "flitted from relationship to relationship," as Steven said, how could she truly fall in love with him, instead of just being *infatuated*? And if she did eventually fall for him, then how long would it be before she realized she didn't really want to be with a guy like him?

"She falls in love all the time?" he asked Steven, gripping his chair tightly.

"She's twenty-four and has found 'the one' six times already. What do you think?" Steven snapped, leaning back in his chair. "But this time she took it too far. I won't stand for it."

He curled his hands into fists, trying to ignore the sinking sensation of doom in the pit of his gut. "Uh, why? What happened?"

"I got her an impossible to find position at a *highly* regarded hospital."

Holt blinked. "But that's great. Why are you so pissed—?"

"I wasn't finished yet, dumbass," Steven snapped. "This position I got her is a rare opportunity. It's one she isn't fully qualified for, and won't be for a long time. On top of that, it's something that generally only opens up to people who are working at the hospital already, so it's a huge fucking deal. A once in a lifetime opportunity, thanks to my buddy Ian down in Delaware."

"But again that's—" Wait. Ian. That name again. That's what she'd been about to tell him the other night. This Ian guy had a job for her, and it was hours away from him. Holt stepped back, his heart dropping to that empty pit in his stomach. "Delaware?"

"Yes. *Delaware*." Steven pinched the bridge of his nose. "But what does she do with this awesome opportunity that I traded a million favors to get for her? She wants to turn it down because of a guy she's just started seeing. A fucking *guy*. I'm going to rip her a new one, and then I'm going to find this guy and kill him for good measure. He's fucking up her life, and I won't allow it. Not when they'll be broken up in a month anyway, like always. Fuck that shit."

Like always. Holt's heart twisted with dread. He'd thought they had something special, but she was the type to love them and leave them. But how…?

It didn't matter how. He knew it was the truth. Her brother wouldn't fucking lie. And *he* was the guy fucking up her life. Here he'd been thinking about trying to make them into something real, and she was giving up this huge thing for him—a temporary relationship in a long line of her passing love affairs.

He couldn't ask that of her, not when he didn't even know if this thing they had going on between them was even going to last, when stacked against all the odds.

Truth be told, they'd pretty much been doomed from the start.

He had no way of knowing anything at all besides the fact that he *liked* her, and she was ready to walk away from a job opportunity like this without a backwards glance?

Hell no.

Not if he had anything to do with it. It had been fun for a little while to dream of happily ever after and maybe finding love…but he couldn't continue to do so.

Not at the cost of her career.

He curled his hands into fists. "Did she already turn down the job?"

"No, I don't think so." He sank back into the chair. "She has until five o'clock tonight to answer him. She told me this morning that she was turning it down, and I begged her to wait until I had a chance to say my piece."

There was still time, then. He could fix this, even though his gut balled up into a fist at the thought…because he knew exactly what he had to do. And he didn't want to. "Don't worry. She'll listen to you."

"Yeah, I wouldn't hold my breath," Steven muttered. "She never has before."

Holt looked over his shoulder. No sign of Lydia yet, so he had time to stop her from making a huge mistake. Had time to make it right. She hadn't told him about this offer, more than likely because she knew he'd tell her to take the job. And she hadn't wanted to hear it.

So…he had to strike first, and hard enough to hurt her more than he'd ever hurt anyone before. Hard enough to make her forget all about him, even though he'd never forget about her in a million years. "I'll leave you to it, then. Good luck."

As he walked out, he focused on the elevators. He had to do this, no matter how much it might hurt. He jabbed the down button, pulled out his phone, and swiped his finger across the screen. Lydia's latest message popped up. *Good luck.*

Swallowing hard, he started typing. *Didn't tell him. Changed my mind. I think we should be done now. Quit while the going's good. It's over. The feeling is gone.*

The elevator doors opened, and he lifted his head.

Standing there, looking fresher than the pure fallen snow on the winter ground, was Lydia. She wore a green dress that hugged her curves, and a pair of boots that hit right below the knee. Her strawberry blonde hair was down, falling in soft waves around her face. She looked absolutely gorgeous.

And he was going to break her heart.

When she saw him, a big smile broke out across her face. "Hey! How did it go?"

"It…" He tightened his hand on his phone, words failing him. For once, it wasn't because of his fucked up brain. It was because he had no idea how to tell her he didn't want to be with her, when he really fucking did. "It…it didn't go."

"What?" She blinked, the smile fading away slowly. "What do you mean?"

He swallowed hard. "I changed my mind. We're — "

"It's about damn time." Steven came up behind him, grabbed Lydia's wrist, and hauled her out of the elevator. "You were supposed to be here ten minutes ago."

Lydia didn't answer him. Instead, she stared at Holt, who couldn't look at her. But he could *feel* her eyes on him. Her phone dinged, and he flinched.

It would be the message he'd sent seconds before the doors opened.

She fought Steven's hold, stopping right next to Holt. "What's — ?"

"Well, I'll leave you two to it," Holt said at the same time.

"Thanks, man," Steven said.

Lydia blinked. "What's going on here? Holt?"

"Why do you keep asking him? He has nothing to do with you giving up your life for some fucking idiot." Steven tried to tug her toward his office, but she didn't budge. Instead, she glanced down at her phone...and made a broken sound. "Lyd, stop delaying and come on."

"Oh..." she whispered. "It's gone?"

"Yeah." Holt finally looked at her. He locked gazes with her, his chest hollowing out at the confusion, and yes, *pain*, in her eyes. "It's gone."

"What's gone?" Steven frowned. "What's going on here?"

"Nothing," Holt said quickly, turning away from Lydia. He couldn't stand seeing her in pain—and knowing he'd been the one to cause it. "Absolutely nothing."

Lydia flinched. "Obviously."

"What the hell is going on?" Steven looked even more confused. "Is there something I need to know? Do you know who the guy is, Holt?"

It's me. I'm the fucking guy. Open your eyes.

"No. Why would he know? It's not like we're friends or anything," Lydia said flatly, stepping back from Holt and tilting her chin up. That one tiny step hurt more than it should have, but it was his damn fault. He never should have fallen so hard, so fast. It had been idiotic. "Let's go. I'm ready for our talk now."

She grabbed Steven's hand and tugged him toward the office. Steven, for his part, looked as if he might finally be figuring something out...but then he shook his head and followed his sister. "Did you two get in a fight when he took you home?"

"No, of course not," she said. "You'd have to be friends with someone to fight with them, or care. He's nothing to me, and I'm nothing to him."

That's not true. None of this is true.

Holt took a step forward. But if he wanted to set her free, then this was the only way to do it. He knew how stubborn she was. If she thought there was even a slight chance that he might be lying...she wouldn't go.

And she needed to fucking go.

• • •

Less than two hours later, a knock sounded on his door. He knew, without looking, who it was going to be. It would be Lydia. He almost didn't answer it, knowing that. But in some masochistic way, he wanted to go through this. Wanted her to yell at him, and tell her how much she hated him. He needed it.

Deserved it.

And then she'd leave him, and he'd never see her again. Or maybe he'd catch glimpses of her here and there, and she'd have a husband at her side. And a cute horde of strawberry-blonde-haired babies. And she'd be so fucking happy, while he...

Well, he wouldn't be.

He knew that already.

But even so, he'd do it. He'd send her away. After a deep breath that felt as if he'd swallowed a box of nails, he opened the door and got his breath punched out of his chest. She wore nothing but a trench coat, which she clearly showed him by holding it wide fucking *open*.

He stumbled back, his body responding in ways it shouldn't have. "Lydia, what the fuck are you—?"

"Oh, you know what I'm doing." She barged inside, kicking the door shut behind her. "This is how I was going to greet you tonight, you know. There was going to be champagne and a dinner, too, but you get the idea."

He gave her his back. If he looked at her for one more second, he'd break. All his resolve to save her from himself would die a quick death. "Well, sorry to disappoint you, but we won't be dining or drinking…or fucking."

"Actually, I don't think you are sorry at all." She came up behind him, stopping close enough for him to feel her heat, but not close enough that they were touching. "So, the feeling's gone, huh?"

"Y-Yes." He swallowed hard, refusing to look at her again. If he did, she'd end up against the door with him between her legs in two-point-two seconds flat. "Gone."

"So if I do this?" He heard her coat hit the floor. She was going to kill him. "You'll feel nothing. Want nothing. Nothing at all."

Jesus. He dragged his hand through his hair, fighting the base urge to turn around and get one last glimpse of her body before he sent her running. "I told you it's over, so, yes. I feel nothing." *Not true. I feel everything.*

"You're so full of it." She stepped even closer. "You aren't even *looking* at me. Look at me, and tell me you don't care. Tell me that everything you said last night was a lie. Tell me to my face that you don't want me anymore."

To be honest, he wasn't sure he could do that at all. But if it meant she got to escape his clutches, he'd have to find a way to make it work. To be strong enough.

He gritted his teeth and turned. She stood there, gloriously naked, wearing nothing but a pair of black heels and a furious scowl. He almost took it all back. Almost knelt at her feet and begged forgiveness.

But then he remembered why he'd done this, and he reinforced his resolve.

"Fine." Looking her straight in the eye, he gave her body a once over, forcing his expression to remain impassive and unimpressed. To add insult to injury, he shrugged. Actually shrugged, as if what he saw was nothing worth looking at. And he hated himself more than ever, which was saying a hell of a lot. "I. Feel. Nothing. It's gone."

She blanched and stumbled back a step. "Oh."

The pain in her eyes was almost too much to bear. It looked as if he'd literally grabbed her heart out of her chest and stomped on it—and he might as well have. He took an uneven step toward her, hand outstretched. "Lydia, I—"

"D-Don't." She held a hand up. Bending at the knees, she picked up her coat and put it back on. She pulled it shut and gripped it closed with white knuckles. "Don't say another word. I was stupid to come here after you told me you were done, and even stupider to think this was about something else."

It felt as if he had a knife jabbed in his throat. "What did you think this was about?"

"I got a job offer, and I thought you were trying to push me away, so I'd go—" She pressed her mouth tightly together. "You know what? It doesn't matter what I thought. I was obviously wrong, so I'm going to go."

You're right. Don't go.

He shoved his hands in his pockets. If he didn't, he'd grab her and kiss her and show her just how right she was. That this was all for show so she'd take the job, instead of taking a chance on a guy like him. One who wouldn't even know what love was if it punched him in the gut or kicked him in the nuts. "All right."

She backed up, a hand over her mouth. He wanted to look away. Wanted to show her he didn't care about her, or what she chose to do with her life.

But he did. He really fucking did.

She almost made it to the door before she stopped. Her hand on the knob, she turned around and stared at him. "Why did you say those things last night?"

"I don't know." He dug his fingers into his palms. "I really don't fucking know. I guess I got caught up in the moment. Mistook lust for something that was...more."

"So all of those things...you didn't mean a single word? Not one?" Shaking her head, she paled. "I don't believe it. I can't."

"Jesus, Lyd. What more do you want from me? A signed confession?"

She came closer. "Kiss me."

"What?" He stumbled backward. "No way."

"Prove to me that you can kiss me and not care." She fisted his shirt and tugged him closer. "*Kiss me.*"

He shook his head, but didn't speak. He wasn't sure he trusted himself to. With an unsteady grip, he cupped her hips, his heart pounding in his ears.

Resting her hands on his chest, she pleaded with him. "Tell me this is some kind of heroic attempt to set me free, or some other ridiculous crap like you read in the romance books, or see in the movies."

"It's over, Lyd. It's that simple."

She nodded once. "Then kiss me. Prove you feel nothing. What will it hurt?"

Everything. His heart twisted. She was fucking killing

him. Why couldn't she just leave already? Anger at himself, and at the whole fucking situation, hit him hard. He didn't want to do this, but he was. And, yes, he knew that long distance relationships were a possibility, and that they could maybe make it.

But he knew nothing about love or relationships in the first place, and the last thing he wanted was a fucking long distance one hanging over his head. Or hers. He'd only hurt her in the end.

So he might as well do it now instead.

Cursing under his breath, he smashed his mouth to hers, forcing himself to keep his mind and heart detached. *Think of war. And pain. And all the death. Anything to stop your heart from warming even more under her soft touch.* After he counted to five, he ended the kiss and let go of her instantly, as if he couldn't wait to move on.

As if he couldn't wait to forget all about her.

Hell, he even ran the back of his hand across his mouth as he stepped back. "Life isn't a fucking romance book, and it's not a movie. It's just cold, hard reality. And we're *done.*"

"I...I'm..." She clutched her coat as if she clung to it for dear life. Her eyes filled with tears, and she nodded. Without finishing, she whirled on her heel, and she didn't look back as she ran out of his house. He stood there, staring at the closed door. Alone.

He'd won. He'd sent her running so she could live out her life. Find a guy who didn't have a history like him. Get married and have cute fucking babies with happy fucking smiles in a pretty fucking house in Delaware. And he'd be here. Alone.

Funny. That didn't feel like winning to him.

Snarling, he picked up the crystal bowl that he'd found in the attic when hc'd bought the place and chucked it at the closed door. It shattered into a million fragments. Next, he picked up the matching vase, which had nothing in it, and threw that, too.

It still wasn't enough to dull the pain piercing his chest.

Chapter Sixteen

A week later, Lydia stood in the shadow of the trees, a glass of spiked punch in her hand and a sunhat shielding her face. It had been seven days since Holt had broken it off with her and she'd made a fool of herself in his living room. She'd been so sure he was making some sort of noble gesture to save her or something. That it had all been an act.

But then she'd seen the empty way he'd looked at her, and felt the passion missing from his kiss, and she'd realized how wrong she'd been. He didn't care, and he never had. All those pretty words he'd said about caring about her, and wanting to take a chance on opening himself up to her, were a lie. Maybe he'd felt them at that moment. Maybe he'd thought they were true when he'd said them. But if they had been, they weren't anymore.

Anything he'd felt for her was gone.

If he ever felt anything for you at all, a small voice whispered in the back of her head.

Steven came up to her. They were at the house of a friend of his, a brother of a coworker or something along those lines. A small part of her had almost backed out when he'd told her it was a work friend, but she refused to cower inside her apartment in fear of seeing Holt, refused to avoid him because he'd broken her heart.

If he could forget about her and move on, so could she. Her heart would be fine.

And if she happened to see him here, she'd lift her chin, smile coolly as if he hadn't broken her, and act as if he was no one to her. Even if it killed her.

Besides, Gianna had come, too. So she had back up.

"Hey, come here," Steven said, catching her elbow and dragging her along without waiting for her to reply. "I want to introduce you to someone."

She followed him. "Oh. You're talking to me again?"

"Yes. I still think you're an idiot for not taking that job, but I get it. At least I know it's not because of some guy now, since you're not with him anymore. But I still think it's a bad move."

She tensed. "It never had anything to do with him. I wanted to stay here, with my family and friends. With *you*, you idiot."

"I know that now." He stopped walking. Awkwardly, he pulled her into his arms and hugged her. "I'm sorry that I acted the way I did, but I have something to make up for my bad behavior. A present, if you will."

She pursed her lips. "It'll make up for you not talking to me for seven days?"

"Don't exaggerate."

She rolled her eyes. "It' been a week since —"

"Fine." He sighed heavily. "It's been six—I called you last night to invite you here, after all."

"Whatever," she murmured, scanning the crowd for Holt.

So far, he hadn't shown his face, but she saw Gianna in the corner of the field, talking to one of Steven's coworkers. His boss, Cooper, stood nearby, too, with his arm around his fiancée. They made quite the pair.

"Okay, smile pretty," Steven muttered, leading her up to a group of four people. Two of them were obviously siblings, since they had the same exact shade of eyes and hair. The other two, she could only assume, were their significant others. "Tyler, this is my sister, Lydia. The one I told you about."

"It's lovely to meet you." Tyler, it turned out, was the man on the left with dark hair and bright green eyes, and he was devastatingly handsome. "I've heard so much about you."

"Nice to meet you," Lydia said politely. "I can't say the same. Do you work with my brother, too?"

"No, I don't. I'm a doctor."

Lydia froze. "O-Oh."

The redhead next to him jabbed her elbow in his ribs. "Oh, and excuse me for my rude manners. This is my fiancée, Christine. Next to her is her brother Jake, who does work with Steven, and his girlfriend, Tara—who also works at Shillings Agency."

Her head swam a little bit with all that information, but she forced a smile and nodded as if she'd actually kept track of who everyone was. "Nice to meet everyone," Lydia said, smiling at the group.

"So, anyway, I hear you're looking for a position." He glanced at Steven, who smiled. "I happen to be looking for a good OR nurse. Think we could make an appointment to have a formal interview?"

This was the second time that her brother had hooked her up with a potential employer. It had to stop at some point. "I'm very happy to hear this, but please know I'm not in the habit of using my brother's friends to land interviews."

Tyler's fiancée smiled. She was gorgeous, with red hair and blue eyes. "Oh, I like you even more now," she said.

Tyler laughed. "If it helps, I'm not friends with your brother. I never met him until a few minutes ago."

"Well, then, I'd love to chat. Especially since you're not friends with my brother." She shook hands with him, grinning when he laughed again. "May I ask one more question, then?"

"Sure," Tyler agreed.

"Is this position in Maine?"

Tyler blinked. "Yes."

Sold. "Great. What day works best for you?"

The rest of the conversation passed quickly, and they settled on a time Monday morning to meet. After they'd changed topics to Jake and Tara—who had the most interesting story of how they fell in love—the hair on the back of her neck stood up.

She quickly found Gianna, who nodded once. It was official. Holt had joined the party. Lydia stood completely still, afraid to turn around. What if he looked at her with cool detachment, or looked resigned to see her, as if she was the one ex he couldn't escape? What if he hated her now, because he couldn't avoid her?

Even though she nodded and smiled her way through the conversation, she'd stopped listening. All of her senses were tuned into Holt, and his arrival at the party. Had he seen her yet? Would he say hello, or turn the other way?

Unable to stand another minute without knowing, she scanned the crowd…and found him. He stood with another man, talking, but he stared at her as if he'd seen a ghost or something equally horrifying. And his stare was anything but empty.

Oh my God.

He had bags under his eyes, as if he hadn't been sleeping. And beneath the haunting pain she could see even from this far away, she saw a spark of life underneath—something that made her think, for a second, that he'd missed her as much as she'd missed him. But that was ridiculous.

He'd broken it off with her, after all.

They stared at each other from across the field, the distance seeming to disappear, and she felt as if she'd been punched in the chest. She'd thought she could stand there and act cold and casual? She'd been wrong. They might have only been together for a short time, but in that short time, she'd fallen for him. Legitimately, head over heels, truly fallen for him. And he'd wanted nothing to do with her.

Stop thinking he wants you. He doesn't. Shaking her head, she broke the eye contact and said, "I'm sorry, please excuse me. I have to go."

"Are you okay?" Steven asked, his forehead wrinkled with concern.

"I'm f-fine," she said quickly. A quick glance in Holt's direction showed him making his way through the crowd, toward her, and she had a mild sense of déjà vu. Here she was, at another party with her brother, trying to escape the same man.

She'd been a fool for coming here.

Steven frowned. "But—"

"I'm *fine*." Spinning on her heel, she took off for Gianna.

She'd only gotten halfway across the field before Holt caught up to her, grabbing her elbow and hauling her behind a tree. His simple touch hit her like an anvil. "Lydia, wait. Why the hell are you here?"

She spun on him, glowering. "Don't touch me. Just leave me alone."

"No." His grip on her flexed, but then he let go. "We need to—"

"We don't *need* to do anything." She crossed her arms tightly, backing up a step. "I'm sorry I came and disrupted your party, but Steven invited me."

"I'm not upset because you're here. I'm upset because you're *here*."

She threw her hands up. "That makes no sense."

"Yes. It does." His nostrils flared. "You're not supposed to be here. You were supposed to go. You're supposed to be hours from here by now."

"Where the hell was I supposed to go?" she asked, putting her hands on her hips. Over his shoulder, she saw Steven talking to Gianna. As they spoke, Gianna pointed at her and Holt, gesturing. "You know what? Never mind. Just go away. Steven is watching, and he'll be on to us."

"I don't give a damn who the hell is watching us. Not anymore."

"Typical man." She snorted, gripping her forearms tightly. "Too little, too late."

"Lydia." He grabbed her hand, his touch faltering slightly. He looked so damn tormented, she couldn't help but freeze. He looked so…so…*sad*. "Please."

She swallowed hard, not pulling free. Steven was *really* studying them now. "What? What do you want, Holt?"

"What I want and what I can have are two different things," he said. He caressed her cheek with his knuckles. "You weren't supposed to *be* here."

Her heart wrenched. Steven scowled, and he stalked over toward them. It was only a matter of time till he reached them. "I have to go. Steven's coming over."

"Fine. Let him come. Why aren't you in Delaware?" he asked, his jaw ticking. "You had till five to accept the job, and Steven said you would."

"*Steven* isn't my voice," she said. "If you wanted to know whether or not I accepted the position, you should have asked me."

"Shit," he said, paling and dragging a hand through his hair. "I was too late, wasn't I? You'd already turned it down?"

"What are you talking about?" she asked, confused as all heck. "Too late for—wait a minute. How did you know about the job?"

"I…uh…" He floundered for words, and she forced herself to wait, even though she wanted to pounce on him and demand answers, to fill the words in for him. "Steven told me about it."

She shoved his shoulders, rage making her see red. "You son of a bitch, you knew, didn't you? You knew what I'd been offered, so you broke it off."

"I—" He tugged on his collar. "Why didn't you take the job?"

"Answer my question first."

He shook his head, locking gazes with her. "No. You."

"I'm leaving," she snapped.

He cursed under his breath, caught her around the waist, and pressed her against a tree, cradling her the whole time to make sure the bark didn't hurt her. "Damn it, Lyd, *yes*. Yes, I knew, and yes, I lied. I lied to you so you'd leave, but you didn't do it. You stayed. Why did you stay?"

"I didn't not take the job because of you, you pompous ass. I didn't take it because I didn't *want* to. It had nothing—I repeat, *nothing*—to do with you. And even if we'd stayed together, it still would have had nothing to do with you. I make my choices based on me, and me alone. Not a guy I'm sleeping with. Who do you think you are?"

"Lydia—"

"Don't. Just don't. You ruined everything. And you—"

Without giving her a chance to finish talking—and she had *so* much she wanted to say—his mouth punished hers with a harsh kiss.

It was as if everything he felt, and wanted to say, was in that kiss. And it hurt, emotionally, to feel it all. Because he'd let her think he didn't care, when he did. Because he'd taken the beautiful thing they'd had, and ruined it. Because… because…

Because he was too late.

Chapter Seventeen

Holt kissed Lydia, every moment of pain he'd felt since telling her he didn't give a shit about her fading away to nothing. Now that she was in his arms again, the world felt as if
it was back on its axis. She hadn't gone to Delaware, but it
hadn't been because of him. She hadn't gone because she
hadn't wanted to move away from her family.

So that meant they could be together, thank fucking
God.

Because he'd realized, over the past few days, that he
missed her. That she meant more to him than he'd ever realized. That he could love her, if given the chance.

He really fucking could.

Her hands curled in his shirt, and she made a small sound
that went straight to his heart. When he'd walked away from
her, he'd thought he'd been doing the right thing. The last
few days had been pure hell without her, and now she was
here, and she wasn't leaving...and he'd do anything to get

her back. Any-fucking-thing.

Because he missed her more than he missed feeling normal.

Reluctantly, he broke the kiss off. Resting his forehead on hers, he took a shaky breath. It was time to tell her all of that, and hope to hell that she forgave him. *Please forgive me.* "Lyd, I'm so fucking sorry."

Lydia pressed her fingers to her mouth. "Why did you do that? Why didn't you ask me—?"

"What the fuck, man?" Steven came up behind them, grabbing Holt by the shoulder and shoving him backward. "What the hell are you doing?"

She rushed forward, standing in front of Steven. "Stop it! He—"

"Why did you kiss her?" Steven demanded, ignoring Lydia as if she didn't even exist. "You think I wouldn't notice? I mean, she's the only one here with wavy red fucking hair."

"Strawberry blonde," Holt said without really meaning to. "It's strawberry blonde, not red."

"Whatever. It doesn't—" Steven staggered back a step. "Wait a minute. That's how you described that girl you went out on a date with a week or two ago. Tell me you aren't fucking around with my little sister behind my back. *Tell me.*"

Holt flinched, remembering all the things he'd said before he realized that the woman he'd been intrigued by was Steven's little sister. "I didn't know who she was, at first. I swear it. By the time I found out, it was too late."

"Steven…" Lydia said, wringing her hands. "This really isn't any of your business. I can take care of myself. And I can answer for myself, too."

Holt held his hands up, but not because he was scared or anything. It was just a measure of respect. But now that he knew Lydia wasn't leaving, it was time to come clean. "I know you can, but he needs to understand what's up."

"What's the point?" she asked, crossing her arms. "It's over."

The hell it was.

"What's over?" Steven asked, not turning away from Holt as he dragged a hand through his hair. He didn't even blink. "What's going on?"

"I was the guy that was fucking with her life."

Lydia growled. "No one was—"

"I'm going to kill you. Slowly and painfully. Twice." Steven stepped closer, his fists clenched at his sides. "How long has this been going on?"

Holt leveled a look on him. "You know the answer to that question already. I told you about her the day after I met her."

"Son of a bitch," Steven growled, swinging at Holt.

Holt ducked, barely missing a nose shot. "It's not what you think, though," he said quickly. "I—"

"It's exactly what I think," Steven said, lunging for Holt again. "And I'm going to fucking kill you."

"Dude, I lo—*argh*." Holt leapt back again, getting caught up on a branch that had been hidden in the leaves. He hit the ground hard, slamming his head on another branch. Stars swam in his vision, and his glasses flew off his face. He knew he was going to get hit, because he didn't have the time to get to his feet before Steven pounced again.

And, he kind of deserved it.

The fact that his best friend was defenseless didn't stop

Steven. He leapt for Holt, obviously intent on shedding some blood. "You son of a—"

"Steven, no!" Lydia screamed, grabbing his fist.

He shook her off and hauled back his arm. This time, he would have connected, but someone grabbed him from behind and yanked him backward. "What the hell is going on here?" Cooper asked, his voice hard.

Lydia fell to her knees beside Holt, her face pale. Her soft fingers touched him. "Are you okay? You hit your head."

He caught her hand, squeezing. "I'm fine. I'll have a headache, but I'll be okay."

"We should get you home so you can take a pill, just in case." She pressed her lips together. "I mean, *you* should go home. And take a pill."

"No, you had it right the first time," he said. He swallowed hard when she wriggled her hand free and scooted away from him. "Lydia, please. I—"

Cooper cleared his throat. He still had his arm around Steven, who was glaring at them and shaking with the urge to kick ass. Holt knew him well enough to recognize the murderous glint in his hazel stare—the one that matched Lydia's perfectly. "Would someone like to tell me why our work function turned into a soap opera?"

Steven flexed his jaw. "Let me go. You might be my boss, but it won't stop me from kicking your ass to get to him. He's messing around with my baby sister."

"*Steven*," Lydia snapped, her cheeks going red. She could feel all the attention at the party focused on her. "Enough."

"I'm not messing around with your sister," Holt said from between clenched teeth. He stared at Lydia, who watched him with wide eyes. "Can we talk…alone? Just give me one more chance to tell you why I did what I did. *Please*."

Lydia hesitated, but then nodded once.

She'd give him that much, at least, but that was it. It was all he'd get, and he knew it. He swallowed hard. "Thank you."

"Hell no." Steven growled, wrestling to be free of Cooper. Everyone else had dispersed, giving them their privacy. It was just Steven, Lydia, Cooper, and him. "You're not getting anywhere near her. No way in hell I'm letting her become another girl on your list."

"Oh, for fuck's sake." Cooper rolled his eyes. "I swear when I fell in love with Kayla, I somehow became the love doctor of Shillings Agency."

"Not her, Steven," Holt said, finally turning away from the woman who held his heart in her hands, even if she didn't know it. "She's never been just another girl to me."

Steven crossed his arms. "Meaning?"

You know exactly what I mean. "I-I…" Holt cleared his throat and took his glasses from Lydia, who had gathered them off the ground. "Meaning, I need to talk to your sister. I refuse to do this in public. This is between me and…" He looked at Lydia. "You. Just me and you. Us."

"Us?" Lydia gripped her knees. "I didn't know there was an us."

Steven growled. "The hell there—"

"Dude." Copper hauled him back again. "Don't."

Steven glowered. "Why the hell not?"

"Open your fucking eyes. They're in love."

"What?" Steven said, looking back and forth between Lydia and Holt. Neither one spoke. They were too busy having a stare down. "Oh. *Shit*."

"Yeah. Exactly." Cooper slung his arm over Steven's

shoulders. "Come on, I'll get you a drink…or ten."

They left, leaving Lydia and Holt alone.

Holt inched closer to Lydia, trying to gauge her reaction to Cooper's statement about them being in love. He knew how he felt about her, but he didn't have a fucking clue if she felt that way about him. It was time to find out, one way or another.

She tucked her hair behind her ear and sighed. "You want to talk? Talk."

"Not here." He rubbed his temple. It was throbbing like a bitch, but not the way it did before an episode. It was because he knew he had one shot at making her forgive him, and if he fucked it up…it was over. Actually over. "Can we go back to my place?"

"Oh. Right. Your head." She stared at the spot he'd rubbed. "Are you—?"

He pinched the bridge of his nose. "I'm fine."

Standing, he held his hand down for her. She hesitated, but then slid her fingers into his. He pulled her to her feet, but didn't release her.

He never wanted to let go again.

And I won't.

"Let's go." She bit her lip. "Once you take your pill, you've got five minutes, and then…I go home. That's all I'm willing to give right now."

He flinched. "Okay."

They headed for the parking lot, not speaking. He'd give anything to know what she was thinking. What was going through her head. He knew he'd hurt her, but he could make it better. He knew exactly how to make it better, if she'd give him the chance. And he'd never stop making it better until the day he died.

When he started leading her to his truck, she dug her heels in. "I'll take my car, and you take yours."

He nodded once, despite the fact that he didn't want to separate from her for even a minute. He'd been a starved man without her, dying for her smile. Her laugh. Her touch. The last thing he wanted to do was watch her walk away… again.

"All right."

As he walked her to her car and opened the door for her, she pressed her lips together and slid into the seat. "Thanks."

Nodding, he walked over to his truck. As he started it, he took a deep breath and stared at himself in the mirror. His reflection watched him judgmentally, narrowing his eyes. "What the fuck are you looking at?" he murmured. "You're as much of a screw-up as I am."

Shaking his head, he reversed and led the way back to his apartment, checking the rearview mirror every so often. Lydia followed him, her face impassive and pretty damn pissed off, as she should be. He'd acted as if she didn't matter to him, when she did. That had been wrong, and he knew it now. He'd learned that lesson the hard way. But he could fix it.

He *had* to.

Chapter Eighteen

Lydia pulled into Holt's driveway, her fingers tight on the steering wheel. The whole afternoon had been warped and twisted and confusing as heck. One second she'd been running from Holt, not wanting to see him or hear his voice at all. And the next, he'd been kissing her and begging for a chance to explain himself.

She didn't know how she felt about that yet. Or about him. Or her. Or anything, really, because her thoughts were all mixed up. And so were her feelings.

Those were a mixture of dread and anger. And hurt, too, because if he'd truly tried to break it off with her so she could be free, then that pissed her off. She was done with men telling her what was best for her. She got enough of that from Steven.

He came up to her door and tugged on it. It was locked, so of course it didn't open. When she didn't move, or unlock it, he stared at her through the glass, his somber blue eyes silently asking her to open up. She still didn't move. She couldn't. Her heartbeat thudded in her head, echoing, and she adjusted her grip on the wheel.

If she let him in...he'd just hurt her all over again.

She'd barely made it through intact last time.

"Lyd..." He tugged on the handle a little harder. "Open the door."

She knew what was going to happen if she did. If she went into his house and let him talk to her, she'd forgive him even though he didn't really deserve it. He was never going to love her like she would love him. He'd told her as much, had told her that he was only going to stay with her until the urge had passed...

Which he'd said had happened.

So why was she going to put herself through this pain again, in a day or two? A week, if she was lucky. What was the point? Eventually, he'd be ready to move on for real. And she'd be left hurting another time. She shook her head and reached for the shifter with a trembling hand.

He paled and placed his hands on her window. "Wait! Don't go."

"I-I can't do this." She shifted into reverse. "I'm sorry."

And then she reversed, leaving him standing alone in his driveway, wearing a navy blue suit, his glasses, and a devastatingly sad look in his eyes.

And her heart broke a second time.

The whole way back to her apartment, her heart raced at full speed. She'd done it. She'd fallen in love with a guy who'd flat out told her he would *never* love her back. What was wrong with her? She parked in her spot and rested her head on her steering wheel. "Idiot, idiot, *idiot*."

A knock sounded on her window. She jumped and lifted her head, half expecting it to be Holt. But it wasn't. It was Steven. Of course it was.

Sighing, she shut her car off and got out. "I'm not in the mood."

"What happened?" He stepped up next to her, his hands curled into fists. "What did he say? What did he do?"

"He didn't say or do anything." She shut her door and gripped her purse strap tight. "I didn't even give him a chance to say anything. I just... I left."

"Why? He obviously cares—"

She blew out a breath. "No offense, but you know nothing about what he feels. Or in this case, doesn't feel."

"True enough. But I do know him. After I cooled off, I was able to think about this more clearly. About how he's been acting, and why. The Holt I know doesn't get worked up over chicks." He dragged a hand down his face. "The guy I saw at the party, fighting with you and asking you to listen, isn't a guy who doesn't care."

She twisted her purse in her hands. "You're wrong. He—"

"No, I'm not. I know Holt." He cocked his head. "But I have to wonder... Do you?"

She swallowed hard, her eyes feeling dry and sandy and broken. Just like her heart. "I...yes, of course I do. I know things you don't know, too."

"His headaches? He told me and Cooper about them yesterday. He said he'd been worried about admitting the truth about his 'shortcomings.'" Steven air-quoted that word with a wince. "But he didn't need to worry about that. Cooper would never have fired him for that. It's not how he rolls."

She stilled. "He told everyone?" she asked, her voice coming out way too soft.

"Yeah," he said, shrugging. "He said he hadn't wanted to come clean, but that a girl who he cared about made him see it wasn't such an embarrassment after all. And from now on, if he feels another episode coming on, all he has to do is let Cooper know that he'll need time off. I'm guessing that the girl he talked about? Yeah, that was you."

"O-Oh."

"So tell me…" Steven crossed his arms and leaned on the doorframe. "Does that sound like a guy who doesn't care?"

I don't know. I don't know anything anymore. She swallowed hard, doubting herself for the first time since driving away, and averted her face from him. "One second you're punching him for touching your little sister, and the next you're championing him?"

"What can I say? I had time to cool down, and I realized if you're going to be with some guy, it might as well be one like Holt. He'll treat you right…because he knows if he doesn't, he'll answer to me." Steven rubbed his jaw. "Want me to talk to him for you, too?"

"No. God no." She opened her door and walked in, blocking him from entering. "Look, I love you. You know I do. But I need to be alone right now. I need to think."

He nodded. "Yeah. Sure."

"Thanks."

After closing the door in his face, she leaned against it and let out a long breath. Sinking to the floor, she dropped her head on her knees. Maybe she shouldn't have run away like that. What if, by some crazy long shot of fate, he'd been about to tell her he wanted more, too? She should have given him the chance to talk.

Maybe, just maybe, she would have liked whatever he'd been about to say. But she'd left. Hadn't listened. What the heck was she supposed to do now? Go back and say, "*Well, you know, maybe I'll listen to you after all. Sorry for that dramatic exit.*"

Someone knocked on the door, and she had no doubt who it was. Steven, of course. He never could leave her alone when she was upset, which was admirable most of the time. But not today. Growling under her breath, she stood up and cracked the door open. "Steven. I told you to—"

The words died in her throat. Because Holt stared back at her through his thick-rimmed black glasses and slid his foot in the crack of the door. "Don't close the door in my face. Just give me a second to explain. *Please.*"

"I-I won't."

He nodded once, but didn't seem to relax at all. "I'm sorry, Lyd. I'm so fucking sorry I said the things I did. I didn't mean them. I swear it. I was an idiot."

She gripped the door, not opening it, but not closing it either. She'd been wishing that she had given him a chance to explain, and now he was here. Like magic. Now, it was time to listen. "Which things, exactly?"

"I didn't lose the feeling. I don't think I ever will. And you're right, I shouldn't have lied to get rid of you, but I thought I was being noble or some shit like that." He rested a hand on the wall outside her door, staring at her with those deep blue eyes of his that killed her. "I swear on my honor to never try to be noble again."

She choked on a laugh. "Um…okay."

"And I swear to never lie to you again. I won't try to protect you from me, and I won't hide the fact that we're together from anyone or anything ever again. Hell, if you take me back, I'll shout it from the rooftops. Tattoo it on my forehead. Whatever the fuck you want."

Shaking her head, she forced herself not to laugh. This was the most untraditional grovel ever, but it was perfect, because it was so very Holt. She almost didn't want to say anything, because then he would stop. And he was saying the best things. "Holt…"

"Life is filled with choices that lead us down roads. And you know what sucks? The roads you don't take never get explored. The choice I made the other day led me down a road I didn't want to take." He swallowed hard. "I don't want to leave the road that we would have lived on untouched. I don't want to be the other me, the one who let you leave. I want to be the me that keeps you by my side forever."

Tears blurred her vision, and she bit down on her lip, letting him say his piece.

"And I *know*. I know I fucked up big. I chose the wrong fucking road." He tapped his fingers restlessly. "I knew the second I sent you away that I was going to regret it, but I didn't realize how much, and how fast."

"Then why did you do it?" she asked, gripping the door tight.

"I already told you that. I thought I was being noble." He lifted his hands, then let them fall. "I swear to never do that shit again. I'm not kidding. I'm not noble at all—I need you."

Her lips twitched. "You do?"

"*Yes*." He dragged a hand through his hair, and shoved

his glasses back into place, his attention focused on something over her shoulder. "And you know what? For the life of me, I don't know how the hell you can like that moment when Rose and the Doctor are separated forever by a fucking wall."

She blinked. "It's emotional, and heartbreaking, and—"

"Yeah, no shit. I learned that." He kicked at a piece of crumpled paper in the hallway. He hadn't stood still for more than two seconds at a time this whole speech. "Because when you wouldn't open the car door, and all I could do was stare at you through the fucking window, I got to feel what he felt a little bit. Actually, I'm feeling it now, too." He placed a hand on the door and glowered at it. "We're still separated, and it fucking sucks. I'm sorry, Lyd. So sorry. But please, *let me in.*"

She tightened her grip on the door. Obviously, she was going to let him in. She'd missed him, and she wanted everything he wanted.

But she was *scared*, too, so she didn't move right away.

He dropped his head on the door. "I will not give up, damn it. You can lock me out. You can refuse to answer my calls. You can burn the teddy bears and flowers I send you in a barrel."

"I wouldn't burn—"

"But nothing, I repeat, nothing, will stop me from showing you that I...I..." He paled and lifted his head, locking gazes with her. "I love you, Lydia. I know it's fucking crazy, and it's only been a few days, really, but I saw my life with you and without you, and I want you back. Please give me another chance to make it right. To love you right. You said if I knocked, you'd always let me in. I'm knocking."

She blinked back tears and opened the door, not saying a word. She didn't need to, really, but she opened her mouth and tried anyway. "I—"

Eyes blazing with determination, he took one step forward before she started speaking, then another when she did. By the third, she was in his arms and his mouth was on hers, taking away all ability to speak. His mouth melded to hers, and he closed his arms around her, holding her tightly against his chest.

And she'd never felt so safe, so *cherished*, before.

He backed her out of the way, and kicked the door shut behind them. As soon as it latched, he picked her up and set her against it, stepping between her legs. Groaning, she wrapped them around him and swirled her tongue around his. As they kissed, he arched his hips, pressing against the spot she needed him most.

Breaking off the kiss with a moan, he dropped his forehead on hers. "I didn't come here just for this. I came here because I don't want to live without you. Because I need you to be happy."

"I know." She cupped his cheeks, smiling up at him. Slowly, she removed his glasses and set them on the table by the door. "I don't want to live without you, either."

He swallowed hard. "You don't?"

"No. Because..." She leaned in and kissed him gently, pulling back before she got too distracted by the feel of his lips on hers. "I love you, too. Have since probably day one, but I didn't want to admit it. I thought you'd never feel that way about me, so I shut it down. Ignored it all."

His eyes turned bluer than the ocean on a sunny, summer day. And the smile he gave her was as warm as the shining sun. "Seriously?"

"Yes." She nodded, not breaking eye contact. "Very."

"I'm the luckiest guy on the earth, then. Maybe the whole fucking universe. In all of time and space and continuum and—"

Laughing, she shook her head. "Oh, just shut up and kiss me already."

Chapter Nineteen

Holt caught her mouth, deepening the kiss while reacquainting himself with her soft curves. Nothing stopped him from having her this time, and nothing stood between him and their happily ever after, so he planned to take his damn time. No matter how hard it might be. He didn't want to miss a moment, a single caress, or moan, or sigh.

Not this time. Never again.

Her fingers flexed on his cheeks, and he softened his kiss. This wasn't about rushing, or dominance, or anything but cementing their love for one another. And he didn't want to ruin it by being too eager, or too fast, or too hard—

"Holt," she whispered against his lips.

"Yeah?"

"I'm going to die if you don't take me. Stop thinking so much, and *kiss me*." She curled her hands into his shirt. "Take what's yours."

His. All fucking his.

He melded his mouth to hers, shutting off his mind. She'd fallen for him because he was, well, him. He shouldn't have to change a damn thing to make her stay in love with him, right? That's what love was.

The person loved you for you—faults, good things, and all.

Slipping his hands under her ass, he cupped her and lifted her slightly so he could fit even better where he wanted to be. She wore a short dress, so all that separated him from what he needed was a thin strip of satin. With a twist of his wrist, he ripped it off, tossing the useless scrap over his shoulder. Her hips moved restlessly until he slid a finger inside her wet heat. Her tongue dueled with his as he pulled his finger out, and thrust two inside, crooking them just right.

Crying out, she broke off the kiss and arched her neck, her mouth in a delicious little *O*. "God, yes."

"Nope." Grinning, he latched onto her neck, biting with just enough pressure to sting. "Still just me."

"Holt…" She rolled her hips, breaths coming out in little spurts. "I need you. Inside me. Now."

"No." He stepped back, letting her legs hit the floor. She collapsed against the door, her mouth pressed into a tight, perfect line. "Not yet."

As she watched, he tugged his shirt over his head. She bit down on her plump lower lip—those lips he loved so damn much. Without glancing away, she gripped her dress and yanked it over her head, too. She only had on a bra and heels. It made him think of the other day, when she'd come to his house in a trench coat…and nothing else.

"Why are you staring at me?"

"Because you're beautiful." He gripped his belt tightly.

"And I'll never grow tired of looking at you."

She blinked rapidly. "Holt…"

He swallowed hard, the empty pain he'd seen in her eyes still haunting him. "I have a lot to make up for, and today is only the start." He undid his belt. "We have our whole lives."

She smiled and undid her bra. "Oh, I plan to hold you to that. You can start by hurrying the hell up and getting over here…naked."

He chuckled and dropped his pants. He headed toward her, his boxer briefs growing increasingly tight on his hard cock. Halfway there, he bent and picked up his belt, tossing it back and forth in his hands. "You know, you almost got your wish. But you forgot something."

She rested against the door, hugging her unclasped bra to her chest. Her breaths quickened as she watched his hands. "What's that?"

"I'm in charge." He cradled the back of her neck posses-sively. "And I say when, and how, we fuck. No matter how much I love you."

Her cheeks flushed. "Yes, sir."

"Good girl." He kissed her gently, and then spun her around so she faced the door. She rested her palms against it, spreading her legs slightly. "You know what happens to good girls…"

"They finish last?" she asked breathlessly.

"Not in my world." He dropped to his knees behind her, kneading her bare ass. Leaning in, he kissed the spot right above her hip. "In my world, you always finish first."

She curled her hands into fists against the door. "You keep saying that, but I'm still standing here…waiting…*sir*."

"That's because"—he lifted his hand and slapped her

with the belt gently—"I'm taking my time. I have a lot to make up for, and I'll be damned if I miss a damn thing."

"*Holt*." Squeezing her thighs together, she let out a strangled groan when he ran the belt between her legs, teasing, but not touching. "*Now*."

"Patience, my love, patience."

Pulling his wrist back, he brought the belt down on her smooth skin again, rubbing the sting away immediately after. Red suffused the pale skin, making his cock twitch even harder. He'd done that. Marked her. Made her his. Held onto her tightly.

And he was never letting go again.

He smacked her one more time with the leather belt before throwing it on the floor. With firm hands, he spun her again and sunk to his knees in front of her. Her smooth stomach was directly in front of him, so he placed a kiss right above the tiny patch of curls above her core. And then his mouth was on her, tasting her, and circling over her in wide, sweeping strokes.

She cried out and lifted a leg, resting it over his shoulder, and jerked on his hair. "Oh my—*Holt*."

His tongue moved over her clit, sucking and pushing and licking until she was screaming out and writhing against the door. And when she came apart in his arms, he was there, holding her up. When she stopped shivering and shaking, he stood and picked her up, carrying her to the bedroom.

After gently laying her down on the bed, he slid the last article of clothing he wore off and opened her nightstand. Closing his fist around a condom, he tore it open and rolled it on, never taking his gaze off her naked, glorious body. She curved in all the right places and dipped in the others.

She was perfection, and he'd never get sick of looking at her. Loving her. Touching her. Making her scream — both with pleasure and frustration.

A smile tipped up her lips. "You're staring at me again."

"Can you blame me?" He crawled up her body, dropping kisses every few inches. When he reached her rosy nipple, he flicked his tongue over it. "Look at you. All pink and pretty and mine."

She curled her legs around his waist. "I'd rather look at you."

"Then you're crazy." He kissed her and pulled back. "Simply." Another quick kiss. "Crazy."

This time when he kissed her, he didn't let go. She moaned into his mouth, and he lifted her hips up before driving inside of her with one fast movement. When she cried out into his mouth, her nails digging into his shoulders, he didn't stop or pause.

He couldn't have even if he tried.

Now that he was buried inside her tight body, there was no going back. Not until he'd come...and made her come a few more times, too. His mouth moved over hers as he made love to her, and he felt her smooth skin. Her shoulders. Her hips. The gentle swell of her breasts.

When he closed his hands over her breasts, squeezing her nipples between his fingers, she arched her back and cried out, her breathing coming in frantic spurts. Her body clamped down on his cock, and he groaned. She was going to kill him. Fucking. Kill. Him. Digging her heels in, she let out another cry. "*I need you.*"

Reaching between their bodies, he rocked his hips into her and pressed his fingers against her clit. She started screaming and thrashing about like a wild woman, and she came again. This time, he let go of the tight hold he had on himself. Growling, he moved his hips as hard and as fast as he could, tipping her up so he hit her G-Spot with each thrust. As he moved inside of her, he whispered words in her ear.

Dirty ones. Sweet ones. Whatever came to his mind.

He didn't even fucking know what he said. "—Fucking love you. I love you so much. Come for me, love. I need you to come."

She parted her lips, a look of rapture taking over her as she did as he asked. He groaned and moved inside of her once, twice, and on the third time…he came, too. Stars exploded in front of him, and he collapsed on top of her, making sure to keep his weight off of her.

"Oh my God," she whispered. "I didn't think that could ever get any better…but it did. You made it better."

He rolled off of her, hauling her with him. She ended up sprawled across his chest, one of her legs over his. "That's because I love you, and will love you for the rest of our lives. I swear it to you, here and now."

"Holt…" She placed her hand over his heart. "I swear it, too. No more running. No more fear. Just us."

"Just us," he repeated. Resting his hand over hers, he squeezed and turned to face her. "You've owned this for longer than you'll ever know." He patted her hand to show her that he meant his heart. "The moment you sat next to me in the bar, I was lost. I'd been trying to avoid people, but you sat next to me…and I was lost. Or maybe I was found."

She smiled and kissed his shoulder. "I almost didn't sit next to you, but then I saw my ex, and it gave me the strength to walk up to say hello to the guy I'd been watching for five minutes."

"Thank God." He tipped her face up, memorizing every single detail of this moment. He never wanted to forget it. "Because I love you, Lydia. I love you so damn much."

Tears filled her eyes. "I love you, too."

He took a deep breath and leaned in, sealing their words with a kiss. It might have taken a lot of work, and a bit of pain, and a huge leap of faith...

But he'd gotten it. They both had.

They'd gotten their happy ending after all.

Epilogue

The timer went off in the kitchen, and Lydia cuddled into the pillow on the couch. It was nine o'clock on Saturday night, and she and Holt were late for their weekly date... with *Doctor Who*. The season finale was on, and he was still in the other room messing around. Sighing, she hit pause on the opening sequence. "It's on! Hurry up!"

"Calm yourself, woman," he called out. "Perfection takes time."

She sniffed the air, and her stomach flipped with an odd mixture of nausea and hunger. A feeling that had become way too familiar over the last two days or so. "That smells delicious. What are you making out there?"

"Apple pie with a hint of cinnamon." He came out of the kitchen wearing a pair of sweats, messy hair—which she'd messed up, thank you very much—and his glasses. No shirt, thank the Lord. In his hands were two plates topped with the treats he'd promised her. "Made from scratch, of course, because I love you so much."

"Have I told you how much *I* love *you* lately?" she asked, watching him as he came across the room. "Because I do."

Setting down the plates, he snorted. "You're only saying that because I bake you delicious things."

"That's not true," she protested. "You're also amazing in bed."

And out of it.

He laughed. "Well...I can't argue with that." Kneeling beside her, he rested his hand on her forehead. "I really shouldn't have touched you tonight, though. How are you doing? Still feeling sick?"

"Um...yeah." She swallowed hard and fidgeted with the blanket he'd pulled over her before going into the kitchen. "But don't worry. I'm okay. I'll feel better soon, I'm sure. The pie will help."

Something flashed across his eyes, and he cocked his head to the side. She still loved it when he did that. "What was that look?"

"What look?" She lowered her head. "I don't know what look you mean."

"You hesitated. And there it was again." He cupped her cheek and studied her. "What's wrong, Lyd?"

Crap, he was on to her. But she hadn't wanted to tell him like this. "N-Nothing. I was just thinking before answering, is all."

"Okay...if you say so. But when you change your mind, I'll be right here waiting." He stood up and sat on the couch, lifting her feet so he could slide underneath them. As soon as he was situated, he picked up the plates and handed one off to her. "I'm ready to start the show, if you are."

She took the pie and stared at the TV. But she didn't hit play. He was so patient and sweet and— "Okay, fine. You're right, there's something I need to tell you. I don't want to stress you out, or make you think you owe me anything, or that we have to change anything. But...I'm...we're..."

"I already know." He locked gazes with her, set his treat down, and he took hers from her limp fingers. Resting his hands on hers, he smiled. She turned them over, and they held onto one another. Funny, how something so simple could make her feel so much better. "I think I knew before you did, Lyd."

"Wait, what?"

"You're pregnant, with our baby. And I couldn't be happier about it." He grinned and crawled over her body, covering her with his length. "Why do you think I brought us both decaf tea instead of our normal wine?"

"I just thought you wanted tea." She pouted. "When did you figure it out?"

"When you started puking every day," he said drily. "It didn't take rocket science to put two and two together. Plus, you missed your period. It was due last week."

She rolled her eyes. "Considering we don't even live together, you know way too much about my menstrual cycle."

"It's the only time I can't make love to you. Of course I know it." He kissed her gently. "And what the hell did you mean when you said that I don't 'owe you anything?'"

Biting down on her lip, she shrugged. "I didn't know if you'd be happy. I mean, this wasn't exactly planned."

"I don't give a damn if it was planned or not." He shook

his head and let out a little laugh. "You're having my baby, and you love me. You saved my life. Made me whole. I owe you everything, Lyd. *Everything*."

"Aww, Holt. I—" She blinked back tears, but it was useless. They came pouring out anyway. "Damn these hormones."

Laughing, he swiped them off her cheeks. "I believe you were going to say, 'I love you.'"

"I was." She nodded. "I totally was."

"I love you, too." He kissed her again, keeping it sweet and soft. When he pulled back, he stared down at her, a bright smile lighting up his face. "And we should fix that."

Blinking, she pursed her lips. "Fix what?"

"The whole you not living with me thing." He swallowed hard. "Lydia, will you move in with me?"

She wanted to. There was no doubt in her mind that she wanted to spend the rest of her life with this man. But... "You don't have to ask just because I'm pregnant."

"I'm not." He frowned at her. "And the fact that you'd think I was is insulting. You know I love you, and I'm going to marry you one day."

The breath caught in her throat. "W-What?"

"That wasn't a proposal." He kissed her again. "When I propose, there will be a dinner, and *Doctor Who* references, and a big romantic moment. And maybe a TARDIS, too. But have no doubt: it'll happen. And it'll be spectacular."

She laughed, and then covered her mouth. "A *TARDIS*?"

"Hell yeah. A motherfucking TARDIS." He mock-glared at her. "Now...are you going to answer my question, or are you going to leave me hanging forever?"

She grinned. "Of course I'll move in with you. Are you crazy?"

"About you. I'm crazy about you." Glancing down, he rested a hand on her belly. "And about this little guy or girl. We have our own little family now, and I couldn't be happier. Because of you. I love you, Lyd."

Wrapping her arms around his neck, she smiled up at him, her heart near to bursting with love. "I love you, too. So much."

"I know." Grinning, he rolled her on top of him. "And I'm the luckiest—"

"—Guy in all the continuum," she finished, before kissing him. And she didn't stop. Because this was true love. Right here. Right now.

Forever.

About the Author

Diane Alberts is a multi-published, bestselling contemporary romance author with Entangled Publishing. She also writes New York Times, USA Today, and Wall Street Journal bestselling new adult books under the name Jen McLaughlin. She's hit the Top 100 lists on Amazon and Barnes and Noble numerous times with numerous titles. She was mentioned in Forbes alongside E. L. James as one of the breakout independent authors to dominate the bestselling lists. Diane is represented by Louise Fury at The Bent Agency.

Made in the USA
Las Vegas, NV
13 September 2023

77529020R00120